1

Every plane flight is different. Sure, the tray tables, stiff seats, plastic interiors, and tasteless fabrics designed to cover stains—those details are the same. But the feelings—where you're going, who you'll see, what the trip has in store—these are always unique.

"Do you think it'll look familiar?" Melissa asks Dove. Out the small window, Melissa can just about see the island. "I mean, aren't all islands pretty similar?"

"Nevis was once called the Queen of the Caribbees," Dove says, not looking up from her book. She's been on the same page for the past hour, spacing out, staring at words but not reading them, her mind too busy racing to concentrate. "But to answer your question . . . no. Even though it's an island, it's not like any others." Dove pauses, her dark blue eyes flashing with memories. "There's a feeling as soon as you land . . ." She shakes her head. "I can't explain it."

Melissa nods. Any feeling would be better than the feeling she has now—the *what if I've made a colossal mistake leaving job security behind on a snowy mountain* feeling. This mixed with a feeling of love lost. Melissa tugs her shirt down over her pale, bare hips and puts the feeling out of her mind, focusing instead on Dove.

"What're you reading, anyway?" Melissa asks, peering over to examine the front cover of her friend's book.

Dove glances at the front of the heavy tome in her hands. In a lush garden two lovers embrace, entwined beneath the words *Romantic Theory: Love throughout Literature by A. J. Samuels*. "A book I'd be assigned to read if I actually were in school."

Melissa wrinkles her forehead. "So, this is for pleasure? What's the point, exactly, of dropping out of university and then doing all the work anyway?"

"For starters, I never dropped out. You have to enroll and go and then quit to be a dropout. I never went in the first place."

Praise for Emily Franklin's novels

"These girls are in for one hot winter as they try and balance work and fun. This series is definitely one to get into." —Teen Scene, on *Balancing Acts*

"Funny and poignant." —*ElleGirl*

"Love tells all in a voice that is alternately funny and heart-wrenching."
—Sarah Dessen, *New York Times* bestselling author of *Just Listen*

"[A] believable, engaging story that keeps you up past your bedtime waiting to see how things turn out." —Pop Gurls

"Wise and witty. So real, so true, I feel like I've just spent a year at prep school with my wise and witty friend Love Bukowski, and I'm ready for another year!" —Julia DeVillers, author of *How My Private, Personal Journal Became a Bestseller*

"Witty . . . wise . . . a good read." —*Kirkus Reviews*

"Love Bukowski lives up to her first name as a sweet and charming character whose trials and tribulations, seen through her witty and keen perspective, will have you rooting for her all the way to the last page. A delightful novel and journey that Franklin's writing makes feel like your own."
—Giselle Zado Wasfie, author of *So Fly*

"Both funny and moving, *The Principles of Love* is a wild ride that gives a fresh perspective on what really goes on at boarding school. I couldn't help but get sucked into Love Bukowski's life, and look forward to her next adventures." —Angie Day, producer of MTV's *Made* and author of *The Way to Somewhere*

"Whether you're sixteen and looking forward or thirty-six and looking back, the first book in the Love Bukowski series will pull your heartstrings with comic, poignant, and perceptive takes on the teenage tribulations of lust, life, and long-lost mothers."
—Heather Swain, author of *Luscious Lemon* and *Eliot's Banana*

"It's easy to fall in love with Love Bukowski. Emily Franklin's novel is fun, funny, and wise—a great book for readers of all ages."
—M. E. Rabb, author of *The Rose Queen* and the Missing Persons Mystery Series

Also by Emily Franklin

Chalet Girls

Balancing Acts

Slippery Slopes

The Principles of Love Novels

The Principles of Love

Piece, Love, & Happiness

Love from London

All You Need Is Love

Summer of Love

Labor of Love

Lessons in Love

chaletgirls

Off the Trails

EMILY FRANKLIN

NAL Jam
Published by New American Library, a division of
Penguin Group (USA) Inc., 375 Hudson Street,
New York, New York 10014, USA
Penguin Group (Canada), 90 Eglinton Avenue East, Suite 700, Toronto,
Ontario M4P 2Y3, Canada (a division of Pearson Penguin Canada Inc.)
Penguin Books Ltd., 80 Strand, London WC2R 0RL, England
Penguin Ireland, 25 St. Stephen's Green, Dublin 2,
Ireland (a division of Penguin Books Ltd.)
Penguin Group (Australia), 250 Camberwell Road, Camberwell, Victoria 3124,
Australia (a division of Pearson Australia Group Pty. Ltd.)
Penguin Books India Pvt. Ltd., 11 Community Centre,
Panchsheel Park, New Delhi – 110 017, India
Penguin Group (NZ), 67 Apollo Drive, Rosedale, North Shore 0632,
New Zealand (a division of Pearson New Zealand Ltd.)
Penguin Books (South Africa) (Pty.) Ltd., 24 Sturdee Avenue,
Rosebank, Johannesburg 2196, South Africa

Penguin Books Ltd., Registered Offices:
80 Strand, London WC2R 0RL, England

First published by NAL Jam, an imprint of New American Library,
a division of Penguin Group (USA) Inc.

First Printing, February 2008
1 3 5 7 9 10 8 6 4 2

LIBRARY OF CONGRESS CATALOGING-IN-PUBLICATION DATA
Franklin, Emily.
Off the trails : chalet girls / Emily Franklin.
p. cm.
Summary: Melissa and Dove travel to the Caribbean, where Dove is eager
to meet up with her boyfriend William while Melissa is unsure of what her future holds,
but when they get there they are in for some surprises.
ISBN: 978-0-451-22300-5
[1. Dating (Social customs)—Fiction. 2. Self-realization—Fiction. 3. Caribbean Area—Fiction.] I. Title.
PZ7.F8583Of 2008
[Fic]—dc22 2007029764

Set in Granjon • *Designed by Elke Sigal*

Printed in the United States of America

For Barbara and Peter

Off the Trails

"Even though you got a place at one of the top schools in the world. Yeah, okay . . ." Melissa pokes Dove in the ribs and rolls her eyes.

Dove shrugs. "I just like to keep up with this stuff. I know it sounds silly." Dove stares at the cover again, imagining she and William are the subjects, kissing. *Soon we will be*, Dove thinks. *Reunited after way too long apart. Who ever said that long-distance love was the way to go?* She imagines the sign he'll have made for her at the airport—something sweet, not too cheesy, just welcoming enough to appease her for leaving her job in the French Alps. *I'm a sucker for grand romantic gestures like that—balloons or flowers, signs saying WELCOME, DOVE, or silly bands that serenade you in a restaurant.* Dove's brain queues up a bunch of scenes and songs, making her eyes sheen with dreaminess.

He'll wave, his eyes gleaming, looking every inch the hot surfer-slash-sailor, and he'll pull me into his arms. Dove lets a small smile flash over her face.

"Ugh." Melissa groans. "I know that face. That's the William Face." She sighs good-naturedly and looks out the window at the nearing island. Rings of blue water, tiny whitecaps, and sand so white in the distance that it looks illuminated make her heart begin to race. Maybe Nevis isn't like other islands. Maybe it will turn out to be a life-changing locale.

Suddenly, the plane angles to the right, dipping down quickly enough that Melissa grips her armrest, causing her heart to officially pound. *My pulse hasn't gone this crazy since I was with Gabe at the New Year's Ball.* Melissa's mouth reveals her feelings, and she frowns. *Clearly, Gabe didn't experience the same rush I did, or he'd have stayed at Les Trois Alpes.* She shrugs off feelings of rejection, the disappointment of admitting she liked Gabe, finally, and then having him like her, too, but not enough to change his plans. *That's the proof of love, isn't it? Wanting to be with someone so much that you'd go out of your way to—* The plane dips again.

"Okay, okay. I'm ready to be on the ground now." Melissa breathes fast, rambling to cover her flying fears. "Talk about a long travel day—I don't even know what day it is." She slides a rubber band from her wrist into her hair, capturing the tight dark ringlets, and wishes she'd brought something to snack on. "Who knew the small planes had no service? What I wouldn't give for a sandwich, a croissant, a piece of stale bread."

"You can get something when we land." Dove sighs and closes her book, but doesn't put it away. "I can't believe we're really here." Would he gasp at her newly cropped hair? Would he look the same, tanned and rough around the edges from boating but with all the charm? Would all the months and weeks she spent pining for her long-distance love pay off? She rubs her eyes and wipes her face with her hand as though she can wipe away any worries about what might be.

Melissa points to the window, elbowing Dove so she'll look out, too. "Check it out. We are *here*. Nevis. Warmth. Finally." Melissa grins. She's read descriptions about the island—its lush foliage, the former plantations and sugar refineries converted into romantic resorts, the endless beach life—but she can't wait to experience it herself.

Dove finally brings herself to look out the window to the view of the island. Surrounded by bright turquoise water, ringed with brilliant white sand, and dotted with houses so massive they can be seen from the air, the place looks at once tranquil, tropical, and inviting. A far cry from the ski resort, Les Trois, where she and Melissa have been slaving away for the past few weeks.

Melissa grabs Dove's hand. "This is so exciting! We're landing!"

Dove nods. "I know. It's just that—" Her voice gets cut off by the pilot making an announcement in French, then following it in English, informing the passengers of their impending arrival.

"You think we'll find Harley somewhere?"

Melissa asks. "She's probably talked her way into some cushy job." A snapshot memory appears in her mind—Harley in her black boots and slim jeans, her black down jacket snug against her frame. Harley always had a way of getting what she wanted, even in situations where she was clearly over her head. *I guess some people are just like that,* Melissa thinks. She's not jealous of that aspect of Harley, but always a little nervous about what havoc it could impose. "Maybe the island life has chilled her out a little," Melissa suggests. "Maybe she's found that the secret to happiness is a cushy work environment."

"With an even cushier romantic life," Dove adds, thinking about Harley's streetwise exterior, her brooding but beautiful features, the proximity that she's had to William. Dove shudders.

Melissa peers out again at the beaches. She wishes she had one of those bikini-ready bodies, but then remembers that she doesn't even have a bathing suit. Nor does she have a job, money to last her more than a couple of days, or a place to stay. A frown threatens to overtake her face.

Dove intercepts the facial expression. "No, no, no. Don't you go getting worried on me. I'm the one in charge of pessimism. You stick to enthusiasm."

"But what if I can't get—"

"You will. We will."

Both winter-pale girls look once more at the island, thinking how from a distance any place can look calm and easy, and as the reality of where they are about to be sinks in, they brace themselves for landing.

2

Scanning the faces for which boy could be the infamous William, Melissa nearly crashes into the person in front of her.

"Watch it!" Tanned to perfection though she's only just arriving, and dressed in Indian-print fabric that's wound into a halter-style dress, the girl huffs as she removes a bit of trailing fabric from under Melissa's shoe. "Ever heard of walking properly?"

Melissa's gut instinct is to come back with some sarcastic comment but instead, she's too busy wondering which boy beauty is William, and how Dove will react when she's finally in his arms. *Hell, if I can't find love myself, I may as well live vicariously through others.*

When she realizes the girl is waiting for her to bow or fawn all over the minor tactical error in coordination, Melissa volunteers this: "Oh, madam, I'm so terribly sorry to have inconvenienced you." Inside, she sticks her tongue out, but her exterior remains fixed.

"Are you just going to stand there and not apologize?" Impatient for a reply, the bronzed and annoyed girl pouts her perfectly glossed lips, lifts her oversized pouchy blue leather bag onto her shoulder, and rolls her eyes. "Guess you don't have much to offer in the way of decency or class."

"I did apologize." Melissa's mouth flies open. She's determined to at least respond more, but the girl beats her to the punch and walks away. Watching her join the throngs of people collecting at the baggage and arrival areas, Melissa hopes this particular girl isn't a fair representation of the other people she'll meet on the island. The girl's blue leather bag bounces as she walks away, leaving Melissa with a bad taste in her mouth.

Melissa rummages through her pockets, flustered from the interaction, and searches for gum.

"Hey, what's wrong?" Dove, breathless from hauling her bags across the sandy linoleum floor, stands before Melissa expectantly.

"Nothing—just a brief encounter with one of those mythical characters, the Beach Bitch. You know the type—all glamour, no reality. Giant bag to hold all her evils." Melissa rolls her eyes, eager to forget the run-in. "But enough about that—what about you? Where is he? I can't wait to meet William!"

"*You* can't wait?" Dove grins. "What about me?" She begins to search the crowd for William's face. The same face that caught her eye so many months back, the same one that appeared in her dreams over the time they'd been apart, making her sure that flying here was the right thing to do. "I'll find him—you find your bags. That way we can just go right away to William's house."

Melissa nods. "Sure. Sounds good." She heads off to watch luggage circle round and round on the conveyor belt, hoping to see her red duffel bag. *Black, green, plaid, floral, ugly yellow*. She says the colors in her head as the various suitcases spin past. *Don't even tell me they lost it.* All around her, fellow passengers claim their luggage and head off to start their vacations. *But what about me?* Melissa doesn't give in to the small panic. Instead, she waits for her bag.

After all the luggage has been picked up and her bag is nowhere to be found, Melissa plunges into the dwindling crowd of people to find Dove.

"Take me away from this place," Melissa orders,

swinging her arms around at the small airport. "I'm ready to collapse on the beach. Even if I have no clothing, no bathing suit, and no sandals to my name."

The small features on Dove's face look sullen. "I can't find him."

Here I am worrying about my bag, and she can't find her boy. "Okay . . . maybe he's late?"

"Maybe." Dove eyes the faces again, hoping for a glimpse of the sign with her name on it, or just William, barefoot and tan, smiling at her short hair. Instinctively, she touches the ends of her pixie cut, fanning the silvery-blond bangs over her forehead. "Maybe he's late. Or maybe . . ." She hates to say it but does. "Or maybe he just forgot."

"Oh, Dove." Melissa gives one more glance over her shoulder at the luggage rack but doesn't see her red duffel. Normally, she would wait and wait and then approach the baggage claim help center, but right now she knows what Dove needs. "You know what? Let's just take off." She raises her dark eyebrows. "We'll grab a cab, head to the nearest beach and kick back with something fruity as we watch the waves." Dove doesn't look so sure. "After all, it is New Year's Day and people are sleeping off their revelry, right? So we'll relax, too."

"And reality?" Dove's voice and face don't seem entirely convinced.

"Meaning?" Melissa asks, edging Dove and her stuff out the sliding glass doors to the taxi stand.

"What about William? And what about meeting up again with Harley, our old bunkmate? And what about money or a job or a place to stay?"

"All very good points." Melissa nods as though she's in a business meeting. "But ones that will have to wait until we have sand in our toes and sun on our cheeks." Dove crosses her arms, doubtful. Melissa does her best to reassure. "Am I or am I not the queen of planning and pressure? Did I or did I not single-handedly pull off a fancy ball for hundreds of people while nursing broken ribs and a very bruised ego?"

Dove gives in. As they step into the heat of the afternoon, the warm air envelops them, sending their shoulders down. Dove peels off her long-sleeved shirt and adjusts her tank top straps. "It does feel good to be something other than cold."

"Oh, you're something other than cold all right," says a voice from behind her.

Dove knows this voice. It could belong to only one person. The one guy she absolutely doesn't want to see right now, having been stood up by William.

Melissa chimes in, "Oh, you mean hot—something other than cool. I get it."

Dove blushes and swats a hand at Melissa's side.

She turns so that she is in full view of him. Him. "Max. What the hell are you doing here?" Dove looks at his rumpled shirt, his similarly disheveled khakis, his too-pale feet sticking out of his flip-flops.

Max, immune to Dove's seeming lack of pleasure at seeing him, pats her on the back. "You didn't think I'd miss a family holiday, did you?"

Dove's face remains stony. *Of course. His parents are here. His siblings are here. Here being taken care of by Harley, the supposed hostess.* "I guess I thought you'd stay snowbound. Or, at the very least, go back to Oxford."

"Oh, you know school doesn't start for ages," Max explains, pushing a hand through his cocoa-colored hair. "Plenty of time for a break at the Sugar Hut."

"The what?" Melissa interjects.

"The Sugar Hut," Max says, hailing a cab. "Family accommodations." He slings his bags into the trunk, opens the door to climb in, staring at Dove. "Speaking of accommodations, where are you two headed?"

Melissa opens her mouth to say they have no idea, but Dove grabs her wrist and covers up. "Don't you worry about that, Max. You just take care of yourself."

Max slides into the cab and sticks his head out the window. "Well," he sighs, searching Dove's face for any signs of like, love, or even lust, "if you need anything, just come to the hut."

The taxi peels off, leaving Dove and Melissa in a small cloud of sand and grit.

"The hut," Melissa says, committing the name to memory. "Always good to have a fallback plan."

"I can't believe he's here," Dove says. Inside, her pulse races from being too close to Max again, too close to her years of liking him, too close to how she'd nearly fallen for him instead of coming here for William. *Maybe I picked the wrong guy,* Dove thinks, looking one last time for William.

"Should we go?" Melissa flags down a cab. The heat prickles up her arm and she wishes she had something—anything—to change into. "I'm going to need a trip into town. Anywhere I can grab a few items to wear."

Dove nods. "Right. Of course." *My boy troubles can wait for a while.* Gathering up her strength and pocketing her disappointment over William's no-show and Max's intensity, Dove puts on a brave face. "I say we head right over to the Pulse, this tiny little boutique that has—"

"Sounds expensive," Melissa says, money worries creeping back in.

Remembering her own financial woes, Dove bites her top lip in the center. It wouldn't be fun to browse and pine for things she could never have, but it might be nice to at least see what's out there. *Maybe Melissa's right and we should just figure out where to go, where to sleep, and how to find William.* Momentarily Dove ponders his whereabouts. *On the beach? Working? Rubbing lotion onto another girl's bare back?* Her stomach turns just picturing it.

"I'd love a shopping spree—even a mini one, trust me," Melissa says, slipping her pile of dark hair back into a simple elastic band.

"Well, this island isn't really the place for a massive shopping binge, but you can stumble onto some cool finds."

"Sounds fun, but . . ." The heat pads the air, making beads of sweat appear on her upper lip. She wipes them away and adds, "But it's not worth blowing all of the tips I made at Les Trois. I mean, think back to all that hard work. You don't want to waste it on a sarong or something, do you?"

"No, I guess not." Dove's excitement begins to flag. What, after all, does she have going for her? No long-term boyfriend waiting for her with a rose or other clichéd token of his affections, no swanky hotel to go to, no promising party or plan for the night or days to follow, and not enough money to fund any of the above. "Where is my fairy godmother? If only there was a way to buy stuff without having to pay . . ."

"Well, there isn't," Melissa says. "Let's get practical and hop on a tram." The pastel-colored trams have a certain appeal to Melissa—the open windows, the jostling crowd headed into town, being on the move rather than stuck at the airport. "Besides, it's bound to be cheaper than a taxi." She wipes her forehead. "I'm going to need a cold drink before I start pounding the pavement for a new job. No shopping for us just yet . . ."

As soon as the words are out, settling into the tropical air, Dove grins. "Not true . . ."

Melissa looks skeptical. "How do you figure?" She pats her pocket to remind her friend of its emptiness.

Dove raises her eyebrows, looking like an excited doll. "What if . . . we charged it?" She pauses, thinking. "To my parents, who I believe still have several accounts around the island. One of which is bound to be at the Pulse . . ."

Melissa opens her mouth in surprise. "Dove, you wouldn't dare! I mean, didn't they specifically tell you that you're cut off from—"

Dove flags a taxi, newly confident in her decision. She opens the door, chucks her bags into the open trunk, and climbs in. She pats the seat next to her so Melissa will join her, and smiles. "True. *They* cut me off financially. But then again, *they* aren't *here*. They're stuck back in the frigid countryside of England. I haven't asked them for a penny since the summer. Nearly six months of self-sufficiency. They won't find out for ages, by which point I'll be able to pay them back with the loads of cash I make at our new fabulous jobs we've yet to find." Melissa hesitates before climbing in next to Dove, wishing her luggage had made the trip to Nevis with her, wishing she hadn't left Gabe behind—or been left—and wishing whole-heartedly that she had a job to give her some security.

"Maybe one T-shirt or something, but that's it," Melissa says as the taxi pulls away from the curb. "But I'll pay for it. It just wouldn't be right to scribble down your parents' names on a charge slip."

Dove slicks some gloss over her lips and looks out the window, her heart beating rapidly. "You'd be surprised at just how easy it is . . ." She turns to Melissa and squeezes her hand. "Besides, what's a holiday without a few surprises?"

3

"I can't believe there are no traffic lights!" Melissa puts her hand out the car window to feel the warm breeze.

I can't believe Max is here on this tiny island and so far, William isn't, Dove thinks to herself, smoothing her short hair so it falls flat on her forehead. With Max so persistent in the past couple of weeks and William so notably absent, being true to her boyfriend was proving more and more difficult. "Not one on the entire island." Dove nods. "You don't think William's gone for good, do you?"

Melissa pats her friend's pale shoulder. "It's a brand-new year. He's probably still at some party or something from last night, and you have way too much going for you to worry about him right now." Melissa sticks her face partway out the window, breathing in the smells of something sweet, the fragrant island air. "Yum—we have to take a food break before we start another round of romantic woes."

"Deal," Dove says and shakes Melissa's hand. Lined with potted palms, the cobblestone street is filled with just the right number of vacationers—making it not too empty, not too crowded. Dove points to a café a block ahead.

"You can stop there, please," she says to the taxi driver, who immediately slows down.

Melissa's stomach rumbles as she watches outdoor diners slide forkfuls of salad and dessert into their mouths, their tanned skin glistening in the sunlight. "Please tell me we can refuel here before the infamous shopping extravaganza?" Melissa pats her belly to show how hungry she is, hoping the distraction will keep Dove from ploughing through with her charge-to-the-parents idea.

Dove leans forward to pay the taxi driver, shoving a wad of crumpled bills back into her wallet before climbing out. "Come on—this place used to have red velvet cake—the best I've ever had." Dove slings her bags onto her small frame and launches full steam ahead toward the café.

Melissa trails slightly behind, soaking up the sunglassed masses, the bronzed boys on Vespa scooters, the well-heeled women in casual yet elegant tropical gear, their shoes click-clacking on the sidewalk. Everywhere are colors: the galleries lining the sidewalk, the buildings complete with gingerbread fretwork in a variety of shades, hanging plants in reds, bright purples, and yellows that trail over the edges of the railings.

Farther up on Main Street the ferryboat lets off small groups of people and then sounds a low horn before setting off into the vibrant blue sea.

Dove stashes her bags behind the hostess stand as though she owns the place and leads Melissa to a table out on the terrace.

"Great spot," Melissa says, her shoulders relaxing. "I feel like my whole body has to unwind."

"I know." Dove nods, looking over Melissa's head at all the people, wondering if she'll see someone she knows, and what that might mean. "Whenever I'm cold—which I was twenty-four hours a day at Les Trois—I always hunch up like this." She demonstrates by bringing her shoulders to her ears.

"Can I get you something?" a tall waitress with an armful of thin gold bangles asks. "We have a great soup, a wonderful roasted lamb with—"

Dove reads Melissa's face instantly. That kind of

food is way too expensive for their budget. They need to make their tip money last as long as possible. "Just your signature is fine." The waitress gives a perfunctory nod and leaves.

"How are you so well versed in their signature drinks?" Melissa studies Dove's face. The girl is an enigma. All along she's been ditching her moneyed past but when Melissa looks at her now, it seems as though Dove is growing less and less sure.

"We—I—my family and I used to take holidays here," Dove says, motioning at the air around her as though she means on the entire island. "Stayed up near the Botanical Gardens." Dove grins, thinking back. "This incredible villa rental—belongs to some royal somewhere who uses it one day a year for yachting or something."

"Sounds pretty grand." Melissa thinks about her own home, the small but adequate beach house where surfing was a way of life, not just an activity.

"Oh, it was grand. Many grands . . ." Dove rubs her fingers together to imply the cost. "Massive bedroom suites, open-air entertaining kitchen, you name it." She shrugs and then smiles when she spots the drinks coming her way. "But that was before—a time long gone by."

"Do you think we'd have been friends then?" Melissa asks, wondering if maybe timing was everything.

She thanks the waitress for the tall cylindrical glass and eyes the drink.

Dove purses her lips. "I don't know if we would have been friends. Maybe. You can't really say how you'd have acted if you're looking back." She wonders for a minute if maybe she means more than just this hypothetical question. And leans forward, whispering. "Mel? What if I made a huge mistake? What if I never should have committed to William?" Dove grasps her drink in her hand, not sipping at it yet. "I mean, what if all this time I placed too much on my relationship with William only to find it doesn't mean what I thought it did?"

Melissa listens to Dove and stares at the "signature drink." Three layers of color—peachy pink on the bottom, pale green in the middle, and bright raspberry on top, crowned with a spear of fresh fruit. Dove rests her chin in her hand and doesn't speak.

"What a sight for sore eyes!" Melissa leans in for a sip, desperate to make Dove forget about her Will woes.

"Right," Dove agrees mournfully, finally giving in and taking a swig. "A sight for sore eyes."

"I could say the same thing about you!" From behind Dove, a fresh face leans back in her chair. "Lily de Rothschild, I knew it was you! Not even your hair could disguise you!" The voice is attached to a young woman with the brightest smile Melissa has ever seen. Dove turns and sees her and can't help but smile back.

"Let me join you." She pulls her chair over to their table and Melissa kicks Dove under the table. Dove kicks her back.

"Melissa Forsythe, this is an old, old family friend, Emmy Taylor."

"God, you make me sound ancient," Emmy says, tossing her auburn hair back from her freckled face. "The truth is, Dove and I used to be quite a team." Dove's eyes go round and her mouth opens to protest. Emmy smirks and says in a conspiratorial way to Melissa, "Don't let her deny it! We stayed up on this hill. At some private club . . ." She looks at Dove to back her up. "What was the name of that place?"

Dove shrugs. "We were at Wyndham Manor. You were at . . ." Dove's voice is muffled by her straw.

"Sugar Hut. That's it! That's the name of the place." Emmy grins excitedly. "What a cool place. Melissa, you should totally see it." She pauses, looking at Dove's drink until Dove hands it over and Emmy sips it. "The Sugar Hut. Ah, the memories. I wonder who's in it now."

Dove looks panicked. Melissa can't figure out why until she repeats the name *Sugar Hut* in her mind. Where had she heard it before? Then it hits her.

Max. Max is staying there. No wonder Dove doesn't want to deal with anything remotely connected to him—or their past.

"I have an idea," Emmy Taylor announces. "I have to get back to my friends—if I can find where they've gone off to. But later, want to crash the Sugar Hut? Just see who's there and demand an instant party or something?" She licks her lips. "It could be fun . . . for old times' sake?"

Worry builds in Dove's stomach. She shakes her head immediately. "No. No, we can't, we have to—"

Melissa jumps in. "We have an appointment."

Emmy looks mildly disappointed. "A spa treatment? You can change it."

"Not a massage or facial, Emmy. We have a meeting. . . ." Her mind goes blank. Who? Where could they possibly both have a meeting?

"With Matthew Chase." Melissa spits the name out, then bites her lip, nervous about lying. In the airport there'd been posters of Matthew Chase, the famous Australian chef who opened a new restaurant on Nevis and was rumored to be heading to New York to start filming his own television show. Melissa had stared at the poster longingly, wishing she could afford to eat at his place or could somehow meet him and tell him how much she admired his casual but careful kitchen ways.

Emmy looks suitably impressed. "Matthew Chase? Well, I guess that's an opportunity you can't pass up . . . even for a bit of fun with me." She stands up and looks at Dove. "Have you suddenly taken an interest in cuisine, Lily? I know you hosted some great dinner parties back in the day, but aren't you just vacationing?"

Dove gives a sideways glance at Melissa. "Yeah, I'm taking a break—but I have recently developed a renewed interest in cooking . . ." She and Melissa lock eyes, instantly thinking back to sweating in the tiny kitchen at Les Trois, serving up tons of delicious food for their guests, prepping and chopping and exhausting themselves all in the name of creative cuisine and good tips.

"I have a fabulous personal chef at home," Emmy says. "Remind me and I'll pass along his name should you ever give up your own . . . ambitions." She laughs, not meanly, but as though cooking for oneself were a silly escapade. Leaning down to fix the strap on her sandal, Emmy adds, "But I mean what I say about getting together at some point. Maybe after your meeting with Matthew Chase."

Dove nods. *There's no way she's going to take no for an answer, so I might as well choose what I do rather than get roped in.* "I'm not up for trekking all the way to the Sugar Hut," she says. "It's old news. What else did you have in mind?"

Emmy stands up, her turquoise tank dress bright even against the colorful backdrop of the café. "Tell you what." She reaches into her small bag and pulls out a slip of paper. "To wrap up my winter holidays I'm having a grand fete at the Botanical Gardens next week. See you there?" Her eyes let both Melissa and Dove know that it's not so much a question as a command.

Melissa shrugs. *How bad could a party be? Besides, it's not as though we have anything else to do.* "Sounds great. Thanks!"

Dove nods and accepts the European kiss on both cheeks from Emmy before finally exhaling as she leaves.

Dove watches Melissa finish her drink. "I guess we have plans. Future plans."

"I guess so." *But what about now?* Melissa wonders. *What about today, tomorrow, and my luggage-less days ahead?*

Dove signals for the bill. "So now I'm assuming we actually have even more reason to raid Pulse. Looks like we're in serious need of clothing."

"I thought you didn't care about things like clothing," Melissa reminds her as she fishes in her pocket for some cash.

Dove brushes her bangs off her forehead, spiking them slightly. From her bag she pulls out a plain light blue elastic strap and slides it on her head. With her hair all the way back from her face she appears even more petite, more vulnerable.

"I don't. At least, not really," she says. Off in the distance, on the sidewalk, Dove sees a group of guys in various shades of button-downs—the unofficial off-duty yachting uniform. *Is William with them?* She squints into the sun, trying to see. Where is he now? Feeling guilty that he missed meeting her? Missing her in the midst of a dream? Or waking up near some long-legged party girl he met on the beach bash circuit? "Maybe I'm not up on all the island info," Dove says, as though Melissa can read her mind, "but someone knows Will—Nevis is too small an island to have secrets."

"Secrets? What's the big deal?" Melissa follows Dove's gaze. She checks her watch, anxious about the time. The idea of not having a place to stay or any semblance of a plan won't leave her alone. *If we don't come up with something soon, maybe we'll have to leave. Or at least, I will. I can't very well sleep on the beach, can I?*

"Just come with me," Dove says, seemingly oblivious to the larger issues at hand. *The whole purpose of being here is to find William, and that's my personal plan*, Dove thinks as she drops money on the table. *A job and a bed are only minor details.* She pulls Melissa out of the café and closer to the group of wandering yacht boys.

4

Walking down the cobblestone street in a pack, the guys look to Melissa and Dove like something out of a catalog.

"One guy's prettier than the next!" Melissa says, keeping her voice low and her eyes diverted enough so she's not staring. None are particularly appealing to her, but en masse the lot of them defines the words *eye candy*.

"Lollipops," Dove confirms, taking the words from Melissa's brain. Dove looks ahead at the pink button-down, the light yellow, the faded red, the white. Yep—candy. "Gourmet jelly beans."

"Custom-made M and M's." Melissa laughs. "Weeks of living together have given you the ability to read my mind." The girls approach the group, Dove giving her trademark sweet smile that causes the guys to slow down.

"Hiiiii." Dove draws out the word to buy herself some time to think of something to say. *Not that I really expected William to be in this bunch, but maybe.* Disappointment looms, threatening to descend on her again. "We just got here and—"

The boy in the faded red shirt interrupts. "Let me guess—you want to know the hottest place to go tonight."

Dove raises her eyebrows and tilts her head, which Melissa knows means she's about to come out with something sarcastic, so she quickly talks. "No—not so much that. We're more interested in finding a place to stay and a place to work."

Clear, concise, to the point, just what we need, Melissa thinks, hoping to find both of those things plus anything other than the clothing on her back to wear. Maybe her luggage has shown up by now. *I'll have to get to the airport at some point and check since they have no way of reaching me. I'll call over soon.*

"You don't seem like the kind of girls who need work on a resort island," one of the guys says. Another nods.

Dove looks annoyed and starts playing with her hair—an old habit. "Oh yeah? Just what kind of girls do we seem like?"

"Hey," says the boy in yellow, "he didn't mean anything by it." He laughs to lighten the mood and blocks his eyes from the sun. Dove can see they're a clear blue, as deep as the farthest ring of the water ahead. "I'm Gus, by the way." He shakes Dove's hand and then Melissa's. After the girls introduce themselves he adds, "We work over there."

Dove and Melissa look to where he's pointing. Stretched out against the rocking sea is a long dock, separate from the wharf that houses many boats, yachts, and assorted seacraft. "Mine's *Sea You Later*. As in *s-e-a*." He rolls his eyes. "Bad pun, but then again, half the boat names are so lame."

"That one?" Melissa singles out the enormous yacht, its windows gleaming in the sunlight. "It's huge."

Gus nods. "Seems even bigger when you're scrubbing it at the end of the day. The good news is that the owner and her guests only come down a few times a season."

"And the rest of the time?" Dove asks, fighting the urge to ask directly about William. *William's on a yacht. Presumably they all know each other.* She studies the boys' faces as though some detail in them might provide a clue about her missing beau.

"The rest of the time is chill," Gus says. "Upkeep, planning, maintenance."

Melissa says, half jokingly, "Need a cook?" She mimes dicing with her hands to prove she knows what she's talking about.

Gus looks at the rest of the group. "We're all on different boats . . ."

The boy in the white shirt speaks up. "That's me—deckhand on *Fire It Up*, the dark blue one by the wood piling over there. Wish we did need a new chef—our current one's . . . How to say this? Not the nicest of people." He shrugs. "But I think we're all set for staff. Sorry."

Melissa's heart sinks. Any slim possibility of jobs just vanished. She doesn't say anything, hoping that her silence will lead to a double job offer—one for Dove, one for her. Then she remembers she hates being seasick and reconsiders.

Gus shoves his hands in his pockets and says, "It's not the easiest of jobs, you know." Melissa can't help but laugh and nudge Dove, who smirks. Gus's blue eyes register his awareness of being somewhat clueless to the girls' inside information. "Why? You know someone who can serve ceviche and pair it with an appropriate dessert?" His voice sounds like a dare.

Despite her focus on thoughts of William, Dove can't resist the challenge. "I serve ceviche in emptied shells, cleaned, of course, and scattered with lime shavings and a small puree of coconut on the side for sweetness. You need to be careful about desserts—everyone has such different tastes—but what I envision is a platter of mini tarts and pies done in a range of citrus flavors." She gestures with her fingers, pointing to imaginary food. "Baby Key lime over there, crème brûlee toasts there, candied guava strips, and so on."

Gus and his friends look suitably impressed. "Okay—that officially made me hungry." Gus nods to his crew. "You guys go ahead. I'll meet up with you."

Still fidgeting with her hair, Dove removes the headband and waits for an answer from Gus. "So . . . was the food question idle or are you really interested?"

"Well, that depends. What exactly are your qualifications—aside from verbal menus, I mean?"

Dove folds her hands in front of her as though about to take a restaurant order. "The Alps—the chalets—ever heard of working there?" Gus nods. "Well, I just finished the holiday season there." She shoots Melissa a look that says not to mention the fact that Dove's "season" was about cleaning the ovens rather than cooking in them.

"Resort food in the mountains," Gus says, nodding. He looks hard at Dove's face as her hair comes down over her forehead. She notices his looking and gets a little nervous. Sure, Gus is adorable, but with Max on the island and—supposedly—William—the least of her concerns is finding one more boy to be tangled with. "As luck would have it, we just lost our cook." Gus thumbs behind him as though the road in back of him leads to everywhere else. "She took off with some guy."

"Occupational hazard." Melissa grins. Gus looks at her and returns the gesture.

Dove licks her lips and shifts her bags on her shoulders. Melissa remembers that she has no luggage and her grin fades. "Would you be up for a job? Either of you? Assuming you have the experience to back you up?" Gus sounds professional and waits for their response.

Melissa makes a face, wishing she didn't have to say the following: "I would so love to have a job. Any job. But particularly that job. But . . . the truth is, I get really terrible seasickness." Dove looks surprised. Melissa nods, proving her point. "Once I threw up all over the deck of my uncle's boat—and I'll tell you the boat in question was actually a canoe."

Gus laughs but shakes his head. "Probably not the best match for *Sea You Later*, then." He looks to Dove. Her bright blond hair gleams in the light, making her appear to be glowing. "What about you?"

Dove thinks about William, about how she

thought he'd have everything sorted out for her—job, place to sleep, built-in circle of friends. Then she thinks how maybe making those assumptions is what's wrong in her life. *If I can't decide for myself—if I can't show up somewhere and make it happen, then what's the point? I've given up so much—trust fund, family, school—to be here, and here isn't even the here I thought I was getting.* "Absolutely!" Dove confirms. "I would love to work on *Sea You Later*."

Gus smiles. "Great. Consider it a deal. Everything's done by verbal agreement here—no contracts or anything." Dove nods, following along. "Let me take you back to the boat so you can drop your stuff—and see your cabin and get your bearings. Let's just say it's cozy."

"Meaning tiny?"

Gus nods and slings one of her bags on his back. "Pretty much, yeah. But not bad for a year off."

"Is that what you're doing?" Melissa asks, her heart somewhere in her feet. *How did Dove, who didn't even care about a job and a place to stay, already wind up covered? And how am I still left with nada?*

As they walk the length of the hot sidewalk toward the boats, Gus explains. "A lot of us are in the gap year—between high school and college. I worked every summer off the shore of Maine so this was a pretty natural thing to do with my time off."

Dove bites her lip. *Time off. Time off. What exactly am I doing now?* She knows the inevitable follow-up question looms.

"And both of you?" Gus asks. He leads them down the dock toward *Sea You Later* and Melissa can't help but be impressed by the sheer size of the yacht, even if it's lacking a little taste and is mainly a show boat.

"I'm from Australia, worked at the ski chalets in the Alps, and now I'm here . . ." Melissa is shocked by how open-ended her sentence is. "I guess I have no idea what comes next."

"Maybe you'll figure it out here," Gus suggests.

"She will," Dove confirms and gives Melissa's hand a quick squeeze for reassurance despite her own doubts about her own future.

Gus stops by the gangplank and looks at Dove, his forehead wrinkled in concentration. "And where will you go?"

Dove pauses. "I was meant to . . ." She stops herself and tries to act nonchalant, shrugging. "I'll see where the *Sea* takes me. Heh." She laughs at her own bad pun. She thinks back to being at Les Trois, being with Max—it feels like so long ago, sitting with him, talking about maybe going back to England, starting Oxford University like she was supposed to. *Maybe Nevis is a sign*, Dove thinks quickly. But what kind of sign? A sign she should forget all this, forget William and go home? Or a sign that she should follow the random path and take the cooking job?

"I have to say—" Gus waits before showing them on board. "You"—he points to Dove—"look really familiar. But I can't think why."

Dove shakes her head. "You don't seem familiar to me."

"You never summered in Maine?"

Melissa laughs, thinking about Dove's luxurious summers at her parents' country estate. Dove says, "Nope. England born and bred. Haven't even been to the States before."

Melissa looks surprised and turns to her friend. "Really? I went to New York once and it was incredible. I've always wanted to go back."

Gus refuses to give up on where he's seen Dove before. "Wait a second . . . did you always have short hair?"

Dove blushes as though she's been caught doing something illicit. Her hands fly up to her cropped locks, wishing for a minute she hadn't cut them on the spur of the moment. Had Harley convinced her? Thinking of Harley now makes her even more curious where that girl was now. Still on the island? And if so, where, and—Dove swallows—with whom? "It used to be long. Very long."

Gus snaps his finger, realizing. "I got it. You—you're that girl."

Melissa looks at him like he's bonkers and feels just the tiniest bit glad she isn't working with him if he's really off-kilter. Then again, any job would be better than none, right?

"Excuse me?" Dove holds her bag tightly in her hand, ready to run with Melissa if Gus doesn't explain his weirdness.

"Wait—let me back up so you don't think I'm a freak." Gus sighs and motions with his hands. "You can't see it now, because it moved . . ."

Melissa looks at Dove, conveying with her eyes how odd this all is. "What moved?" *Your brain?* Melissa wonders, but doesn't say. The sun shifts, starting its hours-long descent to the horizon. *Where will I be tonight?* She pictures tossing and turning on the sand and gets goose bumps. *Maybe I should have stayed at Les Trois. But how could I? Especially after everything that happened with Gabe?* Right now Gabe would be heading for some Scandinavian country with all his ski gear—so far from here.

Gus drops Dove's bag and claps his hands to signal that he's regained focus. "Okay—okay. Here's the deal. The yacht that usually ties up over there is one of the biggest. They made the day trip to St. Kitts, Nevis's sister island."

"I've been there." Dove nods, recalling family trips back when she was younger. Back when she was still a part of her family.

"And the reason I bring this up is because your . . ." He touches Dove's shoulder. "Your photograph is plastered on the inside of the crew's berths."

Dove's mouth goes slack in shock. "Wait—what?"

"You're the girl."

"Which girl?" Dove sounds genuinely confused.

"William's girlfriend," Gus explains, finally getting it out. "Except you have this long hair in the picture, so it took me a while to figure it out."

Dove's face lights up with a smile. "You saw me? On William's wall?"

Gus shrugs. "Actually, it's a communal wall—shared quarters and all that. But yes, suffice to say you are well represented."

Despite how normally reserved she is, Dove can't help but gush. "Really? That's cool because I was just thinking that maybe . . . I mean, William was supposed to . . ."

Gus opens his mouth and gestures to stop Dove from spewing more. "You didn't get his message? I was with him when he called the airline from my phone this morning—his cell died, by the way, in case you've been trying to reach him."

Dove's shoulders relax, her bones feel jellied, and

her heart soars. *All this time I thought he wasn't calling me back or was up to something bad, but see? There's a real reason. An excuse for how out of touch we've been.* "So he meant to meet me at the airport?"

Gus nods. "Yeah, he did. But the captain of his boat is pretty fickle and decided last minute—as in last minute as Will was stepping ashore to come meet you—that he wanted to spend the first day of the year at some waterfall on St. Kitts."

Melissa, hot in the afternoon sun, sighs. "Waterfall. Sounds nice." Then, realizing she hasn't said anything to Dove, she leans in and whispers, "See? Everything's okay—he's still the William you thought."

Dove grins. Gus picks up her bags. "Okay—enough chitchat. Let's get you settled." He looks at Melissa and a look of pity washes over him. "And hey—if you need to crash here for a night or two, that's fine."

Great, Melissa thinks. *I'm the friend on the couch with no prospects.* She smiles to show her gratitude but wishes she didn't need to. "You guys go ahead, I'll wait here."

"You sure?" Gus asks.

Dove, grinning and instantly recovered from any and all moodiness, adds, "It's not like you'll get seasick just having a tour."

Melissa raises her eyebrows and sits on the dock, her legs dangling toward but not into the clear water. "Oh yeah? Wanna see?"

She watches an elated Dove step aboard after Gus, then watches the water rippling below her feet. *If I had anything to swim in—or to change into—I'd just hop in the water right now.* Melissa feels the warmth of the afternoon mix with her worries about where to sleep and where to work. *If Gabe hadn't pushed me away, maybe none of this would be happening. But he did. And here I am, surrounded by water and—*

"Oh, crap." Before Melissa can stop it, her flip-flop slides off her foot and into the water. It floats on the surface, just out of reach. She leans onto the dock on her stomach and tries to grab it, but can't. Aloud she mutters, "Oh, so now I have no clothing, no luggage, no job, no place to stay, and only one shoe? Am I cursed or what?"

She stays on her stomach, her dark curls and hands still angling toward the water, with her flip-flop starting to float away.

"I wouldn't say you're cursed," says a voice. "But maybe presented with a few challenges?"

A pair of bare feet appears in her line of vision. Melissa follows the feet to the legs they're attached to, and continues up until she gets to a pair of bright orange shorts and a bare chest that makes her heart jump further than her flip-flop. She sits up quickly and points. "My shoe." The two small words are all she can muster, feeling as flustered as she is by the situation and the sudden appearance of this golden incredible boy with his toned shoulders, tanned stomach, close-cut light brown hair, and dark green eyes that stand out.

"Here, take this." He hands her a metal pole from the side of the dock. "Use the hook on the end of it. It's meant to grab boat lines, but I'm sure it can manage a flip-flop."

Melissa finagles the pole, only once whacking the guy in the side as she tries to steady herself and not fall in. "Almost. Wait—hang on." She struggles but eventually rescues her shoe, pulling it wet and dripping from the ocean. It lands with a sloppy thud on the deck.

"Not bad for a first-timer," he says and gives her the slightest of smiles.

Taken by his gentle voice and amazing exterior, Melissa stumbles over her words. "Well, thanks you. I mean, thank you. And I guess . . ." *What do I guess? Nothing. I have nothing to say and oh my god, he's so cute and staring at me.*

"I guess . . . no problem." He laughs and gives her a half wave and heads off down the dock.

She watches him in his orange shorts, thinking that their color reminds her of something from the ocean— A buoy? A dinghy? A boat bumper? No— she smiles, temporarily forgetting all the pressures of not having a plan—a life vest.

5

After a night spent rocking on the dockside waves, Melissa emerges from the crew's shared cabin and sits on the deck with a mug of coffee. Gus, dressed in the yacht's crested T-shirt and ripped khakis, wipes down the white cushions and sips from his own mug.

"Sleep well?" he asks.

Melissa reaches her arms up toward the clear pale blue sky, trying to stretch out the aches and kinks in her muscles. "Ah, sure." She tries to sound positive and upbeat even though inside her doubts have officially taken over.

"You seem dubious."

"Well, as I stated yesterday, I'm not much of a boat person." Melissa laughs at herself. "Of course you might wonder then what I'm doing on a yacht and, beyond that, what I'm doing on an island."

"It did cross my mind." Gus sits near her on the semicircle of white cushions, leaving his wet rag draped over the yacht's side to dry.

"I didn't plan on this, just so you know," Melissa explains. "I thought I'd—" She stops short of completing her sentence when she's sure she sees the guy in the orange bathing suit shorts from yesterday.

Gus waits for her to continue but when she doesn't, he excuses himself to go finish wiping the rest of the deck and cushions. "Even if the owner isn't here, we have to keep everything spotless and perfect."

"Just in case?" Melissa asks.

"Exactly."

Melissa stands up and then crouches down when she thinks the orange-shorts guy might see her. *The last thing I want to do is be seen by him looking as rough as I feel.* Not usually one to care about her clothing, Melissa can't help but despise her outfit. "After all," she says to Dove inside the small galley where Dove is testing the stove and trying out her recipes in an unfamiliar kitchen, "I've been wearing this shirt and these pants for how long? Well over twenty-four hours, okay? And when you factor in the time change from Europe to here . . ."

Dove gives her a look. "I get it. You feel gross. Slimy."

"Thanks for the affirmation."

Dove hands her a slice of chocolate pound cake. "Try it."

Melissa bites into it, enjoying every moment of the mouthful. "Okay, you're forgiven for calling me slimy."

"Hey, I didn't call you slimy. I said you felt slimy. Difference."

Melissa hoists herself up on the counter but has to crouch over to fit. The entire galley is the size of a large closet, complete with two stainless-steel sinks, various cabinets, and storage hidden in just about every conceivable place. Dove lifts the cutting board where she sliced the chocolate loaf and shows Melissa. "Isn't that clever? That's where all the knives are. Hidden under the counter!"

Melissa nods. "This room is a vision in design and planning . . ." She pauses, nibbling the rest of the bread. "Unlike my life, which at this point—"

"A whopping day after we arrived—"

Melissa cuts Dove off. "Still, I am without a plan. And without clothes in which to execute that plan."

Dove wipes her hands on the white apron tied

around her waist. She motions for Gus and his fellow deckhands to come into the galley for breakfast. "Look—I have to feed the crew. I meant what I said yesterday."

"About?" Melissa watches Naomi, Gus, and Ben all make their way from the elegant living room inside the yacht toward the kitchen and feels left out, reminded that she's not one of them.

Dove puts her hands on Melissa's shoulders. "Go back up to the street, take a left, then find a little shop filled with batik fabrics. Behind that, in a little courtyard, is Pulse, that store I told you about. Get a few things."

"And I'm supposed to pay for this how?" Melissa feels her pocket. "I've got enough money to last maybe two days before I'm not just testing your food but relying on it for handouts."

"Which is why," Dove says, putting all the slices of chocolate bread on a platter she pulls from a hidden compartment behind the sink, "you should get what you want and walk up to the register and confidently—but not too loudly—say you'd like to charge it to the de Rothschild account."

"Just like that?" Melissa feels a wash of guilt. "I mean, do you think they'll let me? Am I going to get arrested or something? And don't you feel bad about it?"

"I feel"—Dove sighs—"that my parents put me in a really difficult position and I made the best of it and if I want to do this one small thing, then it's my doing."

She steadies her eyes on Melissa's. "Just do it, okay? And enjoy yourself."

Melissa nods.

Gus, upon hearing the last of their conversation, butts in with, "And find out what we're all doing this afternoon. We need a plan."

"Tell me about it." Melissa nods and leaves.

This must be the batik fabric store, Melissa thinks to herself, painfully self-conscious about the wrinkled state of her clothing, her matted hair, and just about everything that comes with not having anything mapped out. She idles by the handcrafted-silver shop with its twisty rings and complicated necklaces that would stand out against the vacationers' skin. The batik fabrics range from deep indigo to muted fuchsia, each sarong or shawl with starbursts of white or colors that make Melissa think of fireworks. *Leche-vitrines*, she thinks. "Lick the windows"—French for window-shopping. Then she remembers her task and Dove's directions. Turn left, small courtyard—here we go.

In front of her, a piece of driftwood painted a milky turquoise announces that she has indeed found Pulse. Stark white exterior walls lead to similarly colored interior ones and Melissa makes her way from the small front stoop to the racks of clothes and soothing background music. *Maybe I could work here*, she thinks, excited all of a sudden. *I could just ask—I mean, I'm sure they don't have a dress code or anything.*

At that moment, three identically dressed, tall, glamorous salespeople emerge from behind a thick white curtain and circle Melissa. "Is there anything we can help you with?"

Melissa shakes her head shyly. "No, just looking." *Or borrowing other people's parents' accounts.*

"Do let us know if we can assist you in any way," says one raillike woman. Melissa can't tell them apart—each has dark hair slicked back in a bun, long legs accentuated by slim-fitting crisp white linen trousers, and a bat-sleeved black top.

I'm never going to be able to pull this off, Melissa thinks, gathering a couple of items and holding them over her arm. *They'll never buy that I'm a Rothschild. Or a de Rothschild.* She scoops up a couple of overpriced T-shirts, a pair of everyday shorts, and a deep green flowing skirt.

"Can I put these in a fitting room for you?" asks a sales assistant.

Melissa doesn't look at her, afraid that her eyes will give away her nervousness at using someone else's charge. "I wasn't planning on trying them on, actually." She grabs a neatly folded sarong and says, "I like this" as though she buys this much clothing all the time.

"You really should go to a fitting room," the woman says, her voice still calm but growing firm.

Melissa insists. "Really—I know my size. I'll be fine."

The saleswoman takes the sarong out of Melissa's hands and holds her by the elbow. "I really must insist, madam."

It's only when Melissa hears the word *madam* that she checks the assistant's face for signs of seriousness. As soon as Melissa looks at her, she cracks up.

"Oh my—" Melissa starts but the saleswoman pushes her behind a thick frosted-glass door into a changing room bigger than the crew berths on the yacht. Once inside, Melissa turns to face her. "Harley! What the hell are you doing here?"

Harley grins, unpinning her hair from its tight coil and shaking it out. "Now do I look like me?" Melissa nods. "So . . . I've kinda been through a bunch of jobs so far."

"I thought you were being the host to that family—Max's family."

Harley swipes her hair behind her ears and sits on the bench, tucking her legs up. "I do like the green on you—very becoming!" she says in a loud voice. Then, quietly she adds, "Just pretend I'm giving you great sales advice. We work on commission."

"Oh." Melissa checks the price tags while she and Harley talk, and feels her stomach roil with the money factor.

"So I *was* a host, but it was too much. They wanted me at their beck and call every minute and that's just no way to experience the island. . . ." Harley pauses. "Maybe the next size? And yes, we have this in a wide array of colors!"

"And now you're working here?" Melissa adds in her own side commentary, "Terrific advice about the shirts!"

Harley stifles a laugh and hands Melissa one of the T-shirts and the shorts. "Change while I'm telling you this." Melissa slips into a red T-shirt and the black shorts, shakes her head at the red—it reminds her of her ski jacket, which reminds her of Gabe (specifically of kissing him)—and then opts for a pale yellow instead. Suddenly Harley looks perplexed. "Didn't you get my postcards?"

Melissa immediately shakes her head. "No. Not one."

"What about the fax I sent? That cost ten dollars to do."

Melissa continues shaking her head. "Nothing. We thought you—" Melissa swallows.

"What? That I'd forgotten you and Dove?"

"No. Not that. I thought you were kind of angry." She looks at her reflection in the mirror and decides she doesn't look good in yellow. *Plus it shows my bra.* She puts it in the reject pile and grabs a pale pink shirt to try on.

"Angry about what?" Harley refolds the rejected shirts precisely and carefully, obviously having learned the Pulse way of how to do things. "Oh . . . wait—you think I'm holding a grudge about those boys? Gabe and James?"

Melissa nods. Hearing Gabe's name aloud still makes her stomach clench. *I can't help it*, she thinks. *I might not ever see him again, but I will always have a part of me that longs for him*. "And you don't?"

Harley laughs her throaty laugh and then pulls her hair back into its tight bun and slicks on a coat of dark lipstick she pulls from her pocket. "I have to get back out there, but listen. First off, I could care less about the ski bums. You know by now I'm not interested in a guy unless he's interested in me, right?"

Melissa nods, but disagrees about that sentiment for herself. *I like pining for people, I guess. Or at least I'm good at it.* She thinks of orange-shorts guy and rolls her eyes in the mirror. "Good. Glad to know we're okay." She leans over and hugs Harley. "It's good to see you. Dove's working on some yacht already."

"And you?" Harley asks, taking the clothing with her.

"I'm . . . not. Not doing much, really." She looks at Harley, pleading. "Any thoughts?"

"Well, after hosting and before this job, I worked in a new restaurant." Harley grins, her mouth twisted to one side. "Guess it doesn't take long for me to know what's right or wrong, fit-wise."

Melissa raises her eyebrows and tucks a sprig of hair behind her ears. It refuses to stay put. "Are you talking about knowing a job is the right one or . . ." She shoots Harley a look and whispers, "Or something else?"

Harley picks up one of Melissa's discarded shirts and folds it perfectly, looking down. "Retail is right for me. For now." She holds the shirt in her hands carefully and looks at Melissa through the mirror's reflection. "But, yeah, I guess I feel the same way about other things . . ."

"Guys, for instance?" Melissa laughs. "Is there a certain someone who's the right fit?"

"You could say that." Harley purses her lips.

"Care to divulge any further information?" Melissa wonders what guy has the presence to snag Harley's attention—if he's a rich prepster on vacation, a student taking time off, and if he's as breathtaking as the guy in the orange shorts. "So . . . tell me!"

But rather than open up and spill everything to Melissa, Harley shakes her head. A slight blush creeps over her tanned face. "This is different. It's . . . He's . . ."

Melissa nods. "Okay, okay, I get it. You're not ready. Well, when and if . . ."

Harley agrees. "I should go back into the shop. But . . . back to your issues for one minute. The job situation sounds grim." Harley smooths out her outfit while thinking. "You like food, right?"

Melissa perks up. "You know I love food. And I love restaurants! At this point, I'd love dog grooming, hotel cleaning, or even retail. But yes, I'm interested in this place you said you worked. Interested in anything with a paycheck. A hot dog stand on the beach would be fine."

"Well, this place is way beyond that . . . but they do have beach huts in the back if you need a place to stay."

Melissa grins wholeheartedly and realizes in the mirror how much better all the clothing looks when she's smiling. "A job and a place to stay? Two birds with one stone. Plus—you!" She hugs Harley again.

"One thing, though," Harley cautions. "Don't tell them I sent you. I don't exactly have the most stunning of résumés. . . ."

"I'll just show up and try my best. That's all I can do, right?" Melissa feels her stomach clench again but this time with excitement about perhaps having found a purpose for being on the island.

"Come out and I'll ring you up." Harley thinks for a second as she mentally tabulates the cost of the items Melissa's picked out. "Did you do extremely well last week or what? I mean, I like my job but . . ." She lowers her voice. "Everything costs way too much."

Melissa puts her hand over her mouth and looks worried. "Dove told me to charge it. To her parents."

Harley grimaces but then shrugs. "Is she sure?"

"I guess she is—that's what she says."

Harley looks placid, her big brown eyes half closed. "You get clothes and I get commission and neither of us pays."

Not yet, thinks Melissa as she crumples up her old clothing and adjusts her new shorts. "Think this is suitable for an impromptu job interview?"

6

"This is *Sea You Later* speaking on channel nineteen. Trying to reach the *Pinnacle*." Dove's voice wavers into the ship-to-shore radio microphone as she waits for a response.

"All the boats monitor this channel, so someone from the *Pin* should hear soon," Gus says, slightly amused by Dove's obvious nerves. He watches as she fiddles with her hair, the volume control on the radio. She feels her heart pound with each passing second. What if he doesn't answer? *What if he hears me but doesn't want to talk?*

"Breaker one-nine, this is the *Pinnacle* Able Baker Charlie."

The pounding in Dove's chest gets more intense as soon as she hears his voice. She presses on the radio button until Gus grabs it from her. "No, not like that." He speaks into the radio. "Copy that. Switch to channel twelve." He points to the dial so Dove will switch their frequency. Gus turns to her. "Look, now you can talk, but wait for his response before you press the button. And don't talk long. We have to make up the guest quarters, oil the wood tables, and you need to restock the galley."

Dove grins, not caring about the binder of information Gus showed her complete with the owner's likes (pears) and dislikes (all things with cilantro), not caring that she messed up the radio transmission, not caring about anything except hearing William's voice.

"And Dove—" Gus says on his way out of the captain's station.

"Yeah?"

"This is a public station. People can hear everything you're saying."

Gus leaves and Dove waits on channel twelve for William's slightly gravelly voice.

"Hello?" she asks into the airspace.

"Hey! Finally we get to speak." The gravel in his voice is replaced with a slow, easy tone. Dove hears this and wonders what else has changed.

"You sound different," she says, looking out at the sun's rays on the water.

"It's been quite a time here, that's for sure." William breathes in deeply, then exhales. "Wait—hold on—before we say anything else. I'm sorry I couldn't meet you at the airport. I even made a sign."

Dove does a little jump for joy and then contains her enthusiasm. "You did?"

Will laughs. "Well, no. But I thought about it. And it wouldn't have mattered anyway because duty called and I went."

Dove instantly feels a pang. *Why didn't he drop everything for me like I did for him?* It's the first time she's thought of it like this—how much she left behind to follow him and how little he seems to sacrifice for her.

"Miss you," he says suddenly, pulling Dove from her thoughts.

"So," Dove says, pinching herself so she doesn't get too mushy and reveal her incredible desire to see him on public access. "Think we'll be able to usher in the New Year together in our own way tonight?"

"Oh, man . . ." His voice goes down in register, causing Dove's emotions to do the same. "What can I say? Again, I'm totally psyched to see you—really. But we encountered a bit of a problem here."

"Are you okay?" Dove suddenly has images of

him being attacked by a shark or capsizing. There's so much to say—what he thinks it'll be like when they meet up, how his work is going, what his plans are for after the season is over, if she fits into his plans, who he's been hanging out with. She wonders if he's met Harley yet. After all, Harley knew his name and could have easily bumped into him by accident or intentionally.

"We're fine. Just run aground, that's all. Coast guard should be coming soon but I'm guessing we won't be on our way until tomorrow." He sighs and Dove gets chills, almost able to feel his breath on her bare arms. "But right away—and I mean right away—I'll show up and sweep you off your feet."

"Roger that," Dove says, cracking herself up with radio-speak and slightly giddy from the phone call. She thinks about adding how much she misses him, but William cuts her off beforehand.

"*Sea You Later*, over and out."

Dove looks over the water in the direction of St. Kitts, wishing she were there or that she could fast-forward time until she and William are face-to-face.

With her new clothing and hair pulled back, the sun on her shoulders, and the water speeding by to her right, Melissa feels as though she's starting fresh on Nevis.

Someday I'll get a call from the airport and my luggage will have shown up, but until then, I'll make do with what I have. She looks out the trolley bus window at the passing scenery—bright houses, leafy palm trees, blooming hibiscus bushes with their red and yellow bursts of color—and tries to think of what to say when she gets to the restaurant. The driver knew right away which place she meant, even though Harley never told her the name—just the adjectives *new*, *beachfront*, *nice*, *upscale*.

In her mind, Melissa pictures the kind of place she might go with a friend for a nice night out. Not too fancy, but clean and cool with a great view.

"Here we are," the trolley driver says. "Isles Floatant."

Melissa thanks him and gets off the trolley, momentarily disoriented. Her legs feel wobbly, but she realizes this is purely because the structure in front of her is floating. Constructed on a massive float is an all-steel frame topped with what looks like heavy white canvas—all perfectly pristine.

This is the restaurant? Melissa wonders, her mouth agape. Her spirits flag as she realizes that—at least from the outside—the place is incredibly high-end, not just upscale but the kind of place she could never afford to eat in, let alone know how to work in. *And,* she whispers to herself, *the whole thing floats!*

"Part of the design," says a voice who overhears the whisper. "Like it?"

Melissa nods, still awestruck by the sheer magnitude of it. "I would, if . . . I mean, I do, it's just that . . ." She turns to see who it is she's communicating with and finds her mouth again falling open when she's face-to-face with Matthew Chase.

The *Matthew Chase*, she nearly says aloud. *The man I've seen on TV my whole life, the one whose cookbooks everyone studies to learn how and why and what. The one who's a legend. The one who—is looking at me like I'm an idiot. Speak,* she commands herself.

"So you don't like the design? Is that what you're telling me?" Matthew Chase doesn't sound perturbed, just amused that a girl such as Melissa might let her real opinion leak out.

Melissa hems and haws, blushing profusely and wishing she could rewind and erase her words. "I didn't mean I didn't like it. It's fantastic."

Matthew Chase suddenly looks bored and starts to walk away. "Oh, you're one of those."

Melissa follows him a few paces down the beach. "One of what?"

"One of those—'He's Matthew Chase—I must obey and oblige his every word and whim.' Do you know how tiresome it is to have your name in quotation marks all the time?" He pulls at his mustache and frowns.

Melissa knows she's got to either make a bold move or risk having him walk away, disinterested in her forever. "I'm not. One of those people," she says loudly. Matthew Chase stops walking and gives her a moment to go on. "I don't like it. The restaurant. I mean, who wants to bob up and down while eating overpriced tilapia? Not me. I barf the minute I'm on the waves. It's like those restaurants that spin around at the top of a skyscraper. It's all a gimmick."

Oh my gosh—I cannot believe I just said that, she thinks. *Why why why can't I edit myself?*

7

After the big blunder of telling Matthew Chase that she thinks his floating restaurant is silly, Melissa looks at the famous chef's expression—half horrified, half laughing. Melissa tries to explain without offending him. "I mean, it's just . . . your food speaks for itself, don't you think?"

Melissa stands in the wind on the beach as a few clouds roll in, temporarily blanketing the sun and making her feel cold. *Or maybe that's because I just spewed my thoughts to the one person on this island who could give me a great job.*

"It's called Isles Floatant," he explains. He motions for her to come onto the wooden ramp that leads to the front door. "Floating islands." He looks at her expectantly. "You have had them, I assume?"

Melissa bites her top lip and shakes her head. "No."

"Oh, come on in. Everyone's got to sample it at least once." He walks brusquely toward the front door and the staff, clad in all white, all step aside for him, nearly bowing as he enters.

Melissa follows him into the custom-trimmed kitchen, trying her best not to fall over or pay attention to her stomach's response to being off dry land. "What exactly is that?" she asks when Matthew shows her a large kettle. Inside, a creamy custard bubbles gently.

"This," he says, "is our signature dessert. You scoop this up—egg whites, sugar, ginger if I'm feeling snarky, chocolate if I'm newly entranced, or plain if it's just an ordinary day, lavender if it's an extraordinary night." He uses a slotted spoon to mound a pile of the fluffy mixture and then places it gently on top of the bubbling liquid. "The heat from the custard cooks the eggs, and then you do this." He manages to pour the custard into a white dish shaped like an apostrophe. "Here—you try it."

"Oh, I'm kind of klutzy when it comes to this type of thing. I learn eventually, but I'm bound to spill with the first few. Especially since we're . . ." She pauses, taking a breath to steady her stomach. "Rocking."

"Nonsense." Matthew hands her the slotted spoon and waits with his thick arms crossed over his chest.

Melissa shrugs. *What do I have to lose? I already foolishly spoke my mind, insulted his design, and appear to have no knowledge of food at all. If I slosh the whole pot onto my new shirt, I'll just jump over the side and swim ashore.* She grasps the spoon and sticks it into the fluffy egg whites, only to eject some of it onto the floor when the floor lifts and drops under her. "Whoa."

"Speedboat going by. There's a no-wake sign, but no one listens."

Melissa swallows her pride and her nausea and tries again, grabbing a mound of egg whites with the slotted spoon and depositing it into the custard.

"How long do I wait?" she asks, looking at Matthew for an answer. He doesn't give one so she counts to twenty and lifts the egg white cloud out and pours some custard into another apostrophe dish that she gets from under the counter.

Matthew leans on the bare steel counter, eating the dessert with a spoon. Melissa places her dish near his and tries hers tentatively. The smooth sweet liquid slides down her throat, the egg cloud melts in her mouth, and she can't help but smile. "This is brilliant. And I'm not just saying that. I'm semi-nauseated but it's so good I don't care."

Matthew looks smug but grins. "And that, my dear, is the plan behind the person. The reason for the fuss. And of course the rest of the dishes are just as good."

Melissa watches Matthew finish the custard by lifting the apostrophe to his lips and drinking it directly from the bowl. "The tourists love that—you know, casual dining elements mixed with haute cuisine . . ."

"All the same," Melissa says, negging the idea of slurping from the bowl, "I think I'll quit while I'm ahead." She puts her bowl and spoon down.

"Quit?" Matthew's voice is as animated as it is on television. If Melissa closes her eyes for one second she can imagine she's home in her parents' living room listening to him on air. "Why quit when I haven't even hired you yet?"

Melissa clears her dishes and his out of habit, then stands with her hands full, wondering where the sink is. She knows her cheeks are betraying her attempts at a cool demeanor.

"How did you know I was looking for a job? Do I scream *desperate*?" She finally finds the sink and casts a weary gaze toward the chef.

"Not exactly a scream. More like a whisper." He waves at the air. "Not to worry—it'll pass with experience. Same thing with love. I used to give off an air of neediness that sent the ladies running in the opposite direction. Then I realized if I adapted my kitchen confidence to love I wouldn't be alone."

Melissa wonders where all this is leading, if he's giving free romantic advice or hiring. Or both. "And did it work?"

He displays his left hand. "Married for nearly twenty-five years."

Melissa nods, remembering his bio on the flaps of the many cookbooks she's seen—one daughter, one son, happily married, world travel. "And you're about to have a cooking show?" Melissa doesn't realize until she notes his surprised face that maybe this isn't public knowledge. What was that girl's name? Emmy Taylor, Dove's old friend, had mentioned it. "Sorry to pry."

Matthew disregards it. "Yes, in fact. Or—rephrase that—I might. We might if . . ." he sighs, looking frustrated. "If my errant son ever comes around to the idea."

Melissa nods, recalling an interview she read once in a glossy magazine about Matthew Chase, known affectionately as Matty, in which he had spoken about his daughter's business sense and his son's lackadaisical attitude toward the restaurant industry. Without the focus of the food preparation, she feels her legs start to sway again. "So . . ."

Matthew begins assembling a plate of brightly colored fruits and gives signals to waitstaff, who appear as though out of nowhere. "Start tomorrow. Front of the house or back." He raises his neatly trimmed eyebrows and pulls on his mustache, then explains. "Kitchen or waiter—your choice."

Melissa rushes to him and shakes his hand. His laughter tells her he finds her charming. "Thanks! Thank you so much. You have no idea how much I wanted a job. Needed, not wanted."

Matty chuckles and checks an item off his clipboard. The kitchen starts to hum with activity: salad prep work, careful slicing of melon and guava, sauces, and dish washing. "Remember what I said—don't seem desperate. Just be." He breathes in with his eyes closed. "Very Zen."

Melissa tries it. "Okay . . ."

"And don't think just because you aced the rather unconventional interview that you don't have to work." He points to her with his pencil, clicking it on the clipboard. "It's like I always tell my son. You have to show what you can do, not just say it."

"I will," Melissa says. She glances around the large room, wondering what her role will be. Then she remembers her housing options and that Harley had said there were accommodations available. "Um . . . not to push my luck or anything, but you wouldn't know where a new employee might find a place to stay?" Melissa's body thumps with the possibility of solving her woes in one day—clothing, job, bed.

Matty's mouth twists, his eyebrows pull down as though his whole face is a frown, and then he yells an order over his shoulder about freezing some lemons. "That, I'm afraid, is out of my hands." Melissa nods and begins to walk away.

"It's only . . . I'm kind of stuck," Melissa says under her breath.

"Just ask around," Matty says. "You never know who might have a place to rent."

8

"Where are we going, exactly?" Dove asks. Melissa leans forward in the van so she can hear the answer over the heavy wind. Blowing into the vehicle, the night air brings gusts of wind that whoosh and swirl, causing excitement to bubble up around them. The day had been extraordinarily hot. The tarmac had seemed soft under Melissa's feet as she went to work for the first time, showing up at Isles Floatant expecting to wait tables or prepare gourmet food only to find she'd been given the task of peeling, slicing lengthwise, and freezing entire crates of bananas. Her arms ached and her feet were sore, but she felt glad she had a job. A place to stay, however, hadn't happened. *I've asked everyone if they have a place, but no one does,* she'd reported back to Dove.

"You'll see when we get there," Gus says. "I'm just following the van in front, anyway."

Melissa can tell from his eyes that he's kidding, though there is another van in front and, in front of that, a few cars filled with boat crew and vacationers all around their ages. "So you have no idea where this winding road leads?" she asks.

"Nope!"

"So why'd you insist that we wear our bathing suits in the dark?" Dove inquires, trying to get over the fact that her reuniting with William didn't happen in the morning due to further boat problems. *I want to see you so badly*, he'd said into the radio again. But when the *Pinnacle* had run aground because of an out-of-date depth chart, the bottom of the boat had suffered and it needed further repairs. *I'll be there tomorrow,* William had promised.

"I don't know how much more I can take of this waiting and waiting," Dove says to Melissa in the breezy van.

"It's just one more night," Melissa says. "You can do it. Think of the reward."

Dove nods, but feels the familiar doubts rush back. "We'll see, I guess."

"At least you're not wondering where your next night of sleep will come from," Melissa says. "I've asked everywhere! It's not like I can afford one of the luxury suites at the resorts."

"I wish you could keep staying on board with us," Dove says, loudly enough that Gus hears.

"But she can't." His voice is firm. "The owner's coming in a few days and she'll figure it out. We can't risk it. Sorry."

Melissa shrugs, trying to appear casual. Against her better judgment she borrowed a bathing suit from Dove. In the excitement they shared while both told about their workdays—Dove's in the tiny kitchen, Melissa's in the enormous one—borrowing the small suit seemed like a good idea. But now, in the rushing dark, Melissa is fully aware of how differently she and Dove are built. The suit's straps cut into her shoulders and the legs into her thighs. *At work tomorrow I'll buy a cheap suit from a cart near the beach. In the meantime, I'm not planning on going swimming anyway.* "No big deal, right? I'll just ask around tonight . . . wherever it is we're headed."

The van speeds forward on the dark road, then slows as it edges its way up a steep hill.

"From Charlestown we just go south on Main Street," Gus says. His words evaporate into the air. "Almost there."

The van pulls to a stop amid a crowd of other cars, mopeds, and people, all standing around talking and laughing.

"This is it?" Melissa asks as she climbs out of the van.

"No," Dove says, realizing where they are as she looks around. She pulls Melissa over to a steep-edged cliff from which stone steps descend. "That is it."

"Whoa." Melissa stares down at a vast stone pool. Steam rises from the dark water into the blue-tinted air.

"Hot thermal springs!" Gus says excitedly and trots down the steep steps after a group of bikini-clad girls.

"You want to go in?" Melissa asks Dove, hoping she'll say no so the issue of the too-tight bathing suit won't come to light.

"Absolutely." Dove nods. "I was here once years ago and my parents thought it was improper to shed my clothing . . . so I didn't get to go. Come on."

Melissa and Dove take the steps carefully, stopping to look at the ocean far off to their right, moonlight shimmering on its surface. Random voices float up to them, each of the steaming pools seeming to have a different crowd in and around it.

"Let's find a quiet spot," Melissa says once they're on the grass.

"I have to change," Dove says. She plucks at her shirt and shorts.

"Why didn't you do it back at the boat? You practically shoved me into this suit." Melissa groans as she lifts her shirt partway to display Dove's suit.

"You wanted it. I had no intention of swimming so I just brought a one-piece. Navy blue. Trimmed in white. Very tasteful."

Melissa smirks, dreading the moment when she has to strip down. "I'm sure your parents would be proud."

Dove wrinkles her lips and looks around. "Hey, it looks like they've added a few things since the last time I was here." She gestures with her chin. "Changing rooms, massage huts—check those out."

Melissa follows Dove's gaze and sees the wooden changing areas, a few brightly colored small tents with massage tables inside, and then, something—or someone—that Dove didn't point out. "Isn't that . . ."

"Max," Dove says as he strides over to them, shirtless in the breezy night, his physique as glorious as ever.

Melissa watches Dove's face for signs of surprise, but she appears calm. *So he's here, so what?* Dove thinks, focusing on a particularly tall palm tree in the distance to avoid making eye contact with Max. *Just because he's here doesn't mean I have to talk to him.*

"Dove?" Melissa touches her shoulder. "I'm going to find that quiet spot we talked about, okay? Just change and come find me."

Dove crosses her arms over her chest and then rethinks the gesture, wondering if it's too defensive. *After all, what do I have to prove? Nothing.* She fiddles with the bathing suit in her hands.

"Are you annoyed that I'm here?" Max jumps right in.

Dove puts one flip-flop-clad foot on a wooden bench that overlooks the steaming pools. "Is that a question you really want answered?"

Max tilts his head and sits on the bench, his wet skin glistening in the moon rays. "After everything that's gone on between us, yes."

Dove lowers her voice and sits on the other end of the bench from Max. "I guess I am. I mean, I left Les Trois and I thought you were staying. It's not a difficult assumption to make."

Max laughs sarcastically. "Did you ever stop to think that maybe you wanted to make that assumption because it's easier for you?"

Dove clenches her jaw. She thinks about being at school with Max, about wanting him to want her, about their friendship, about how he kissed her ex-best friend, Claire. "Easier than what?"

"Easier than doing what you're going to have to do now."

Dove turns so she has a clear view of Max. Max in the snow. Max in the moonlight. Max the temptation that threatened to get her to betray William. "And what, exactly, do I have to do now?"

Max puts one hand on Dove's bare thigh. "You had William at Les Trois without me. You had me at Les Trois without him. Now you have both of us in the same place at the same time." Max's bright green eyes are magnets for Dove's. She locks her gaze to his, her hands shaking so much that she can't fiddle with the bathing suit or anything else.

"And?" Dove asks but she knows the answer. *Tomorrow, William and I will see each other for the first time in ages. What if it's not the same? What if it's not as good? Or, what if it's even better?* She looks at Max. *And what if I never saw Max again? What would that be like?*

"And I think—before I head back to Oxford—I'd like to know for sure one way or the other." He keeps his hand on her, tenderly but firm, and speaks in a calm voice. "If you like him, I mean really truly do, I'll vanish." He removes his hand and looks at the shimmering ocean water. "And if, on the off chance you decide you can't live without me . . ." He cracks a smile and looks at her, semi-joking and half serious. "Then tell him."

Dove stands up, her hands still shaking. "So that's it?" Max nods. She thinks she'll feel angry with Max. Or angry that William isn't here. Or anything other than what she does. "I guess it makes sense." She stares at him. Max or William. No pretending, no second-guessing. Just figuring it out.

9

Having left Dove and Max to talk, Melissa heads toward the massage huts to investigate.

"The price list is over there," says a woman dressed all in white. "Are you tense? Could you benefit from a Swedish-style relaxing massage?"

"I'm sure I could." Melissa smiles. *Only my wallet won't allow for it. Oh well, at least the thermal hot springs are free.* She walks behind the huts and finds a little clearing in which one of the smaller pools is framed by verdant foliage.

Checking first to see that no one is nearby, Melissa sheds her clothing and tests the water, dipping a toe in. The heat feels intense.

"Ouch. Hot!" Melissa says aloud.

"Yeah, the temps range from 104 to 108," a guy says.

Melissa looks up from where her toe is poised and, upon seeing none other than the hot guy she'd noticed on the dock wearing orange shorts, she is horrified to be bursting out of her—Dove's—swimsuit. "Well, that's my kind of temperature!" She quickly and immediately slips into the water, immersing herself in steaming liquid. At first it stings her skin, making her want to jump out and run for the jungled woods or at the very least cloak herself in a towel. She closes her eyes.

"Feel good?" the orange-shorts guy asks.

Melissa opens her eyes and finds herself directly opposite him in the six-foot-wide pool. "At first it hurt, but now it kind of feels good." Being in the water sets her at ease, despite the fact that she's in such close proximity to the first guy since Gabe to set her heart on its own rhythm.

She can barely see the boy's face in the semidarkness. It's freeing to be in the water, she thinks. Like hiding. They begin to speak, first about the hot springs, then about the island, about their hometowns.

"So, you're part American, part Aussie?" she asks.

"Yep. And you're fully from down under?"

"You sound like a tourist saying that," Melissa scolds. She flicks her hands in the water and wonders where Dove is, if she and Max are shouting or reconciled.

"I'm a tourist of everywhere," he says. He dips all the way under the steamy water and emerges a little closer to Melissa, resting his back against the smooth stone wall.

"And what does that mean, exactly?"

"Just that I'm from all over, lived all over, so while I feel comfortable pretty much everywhere, I don't ever feel fully at home." He puts his mouth to the water and blows bubbles. "Sorry—was that too much of a confession?"

Melissa sinks so that only her face and hair are out of the water, her ill-fitting outfit fully covered. "I like confessions."

They sit in easy silence for a few minutes, hearing laughter and raucous shouts from over the hedges but not leaving their pool to investigate.

"This water makes my blood race, I think," Melissa says, and doesn't regret letting a personal thought leak out. After all, it's true. She rubs her arms, feeling the cool air on her skin and then, suddenly, hoping the guy leaves before she has to, lest he be privy to her borrowed suit.

"Don't you want to meet up with a friend or

something?" Melissa volunteers, unsure which answer she hopes he'll give.

"You trying to get rid of me?" Hoisting himself out of the water, the guy sits on the edge of the pool, watching a couple of other bathers walk by in towels.

Melissa moves closer to him. "No, no. Not like that. Only . . ."

An awkward moment surfaces. *He thinks I'm not interested in . . . whatever he's interested in—talking, hanging out.* "Stay. It's fine."

He laughs and points to the ENTER AT YOUR OWN RISK sign. "Is your heart okay?" the guy asks.

Feeling her pulse speed up right as he says that, Melissa slicks her hair back with some water and nods even though her heartbeats per minute are definitely up. Being near him is a rush. The hot springs are new and different. "Fine . . ."

He slides back into the hot water, meeting her at one of the corners of the pool so they are perpendicular to each other. "Look—let's not do what people usually do in this type of situation."

Melissa reels through the possibilities and asks, "Wait—clarify that."

"Look, we're all young. We're all on vacation."

"I'm not—I'm working," Melissa says defensively.

"Oh, right now?" He looks amused.

"No, not at present, but I will be in a few short

hours. Mere moments and I'll be slaving away chopping chestnuts or honing my skills as a zester of all things citrus."

The guy rolls his eyes and raises his hands. "Enough talk of food. I still have a full stomach from dinner."

"Fine." Melissa grins, enjoying the repartee. "Explain what you mean."

"Say we were back home—wherever that place is in your mind. You meet, you exchange a few snarky lines, and then choose." He points left with one finger. "This way leads to the random hookup."

"And this way?" Melissa asks, still grinning, and pointing in the opposite direction.

"That way leads to 'Can I meet your friend?' "

Melissa sighs. "If you saw me arrive with my friend, Dove, you should know—she's off-limits. She's got a boyfriend." *Of course his interest is piqued by sweet, blond Dove. Not the one who borrows her suit. Not that I care anyway, right?*

The guy shakes his head and reaches an arm out onto the stone wall so it nearly touches Melissa's. "No, wait, that's not what I mean." He lets a noise out through his lips that sounds like a tire expelling air. "Let's just use this—forgive the lame attempt at poetry—veil of night to just say whatever it is that comes to mind."

Melissa absorbs his words and nods. "Okay. So . . . no introductions, no formalities, no need to proclaim feelings or phone numbers?"

"Exactly." He rests his palms on top of the water's surface, feeling its heat.

They sit not saying anything until Melissa cracks up. "Well, this is going well." She tugs at her straps, wishing she could pull them off to stop their cutting into her.

The guy looks around. *Oh, great, now he does want to leave,* Melissa thinks. *The only guy on this island who has caught my eye so far, and I'm scaring him away*. "So, my uncle once passed out at a hot springs."

The tension breaks and he stares at her, listening. "Oh yeah?"

"True. Some people freak out. That's why all the signs say enter at your own risk . . ." Melissa finds herself blathering away, not editing her rambling words. "Especially if you have heart problems—which I do, but not in the way that the people who posted the signs mean."

He leans back against the wall, slinging both arms onto it, exposing his shoulders. "Well, what are yours?"

Melissa watches him, enjoying each ticking second with him, wondering if he knows they'd spoken before on the dock. *I could tell him*, she thinks. *Or will that go back to what he was saying about typical situations?* She decides against it, preferring instead the anonymity they've established. "My what?"

"Your heart problems." He cups his hand in the pool, squirting water up like a whale's spout.

"Oh . . . nothing." Melissa balks at the idea of spilling her woes—her time in the Alps with Gabe that amounted to his leaving her. *Even spying this guy from afar sounds lame if I say it out loud.*

"Your face doesn't make it seem like nothing."

"It's just—it sounds clichéd." Melissa thinks back to her first kiss with Gabe, on top of a mountain in the snow—a million miles away from here, it seems. He was just a guy. A guy she knew and wouldn't see again unless she happened to show up in Norway or Sweden or Austria. Considering her tropical whereabouts, unlikely.

"Do you really believe that or are you just saying it to gloss over murky water?" He pulls himself all the way out of the water, gives her the one-minute sign, grabs something from the massage hut and sprints back, his feet making slapping sounds on the stone. "Here." He hands her a tall plastic glass filled with water.

"Is this pink?" she asks.

"Yes. Rose water and hibiscus tea. Made special for the hot springs."

"Aren't you just a veritable fountain of knowledge?" Melissa sips at the drink, then pauses. "How do I know you didn't spike this or do something evil?"

He removes her fingers from the glass, giving her the briefest experience of skin-to-skin contact with him, then takes a big swig. "Satisfied?" He looks at her. "I'm not a creep."

"So how do you know what this concoction is?"

For the first time, he looks caught off guard. He chews his lower lip and pauses. "Just a good guess, I suppose." He dips his foot in the springs and then plunges in again. When he resurfaces he adds, "And don't for a second think I've forgotten about you glossing over your heartache issues." He waves to a few people walking by.

Melissa looks at them, thinking she recognizes a laugh. She looks deeper into the darkness and shouts, "Harley?"

Through the dimly lit air, Harley waves, smiles, and points to the back of a guy wearing knee-length tropical print shorts and no shirt and holding a hula hoop. With her excited bounce and grasp on the guy's shoulder, she makes it clear to Melissa that this is the guy she was talking about—or was refusing to speak of—at Pulse. As Harley, the guy, and a small group of people head to one of the more remote spring pools, the guy slings his arm around Harley and kisses her cheek. Melissa takes a good look at this boy, his easy stride, his hair—bright blond at the ends even in the dark—and wonders what about him makes Harley so into him. They disappear into the thick brush.

"I guess you can't ever really figure out what makes someone like one person and the next person like someone else," Melissa says, speaking so softly it's almost as though she's talking to herself.

Her water companion sloshes through the steamy pool and considers this. "This sounds like the kind of statement you make when you can't quite deal with love, lust, or anything in that genre." He swipes his wet hands through his hair, drawing attention to smooth skin on his forehead, the gleam in his clear eyes. He looks at Melissa. "Are you over something, under something, or trying to be?"

It's true, Melissa says, trying out the sensation. *Gabe was just a guy. And it's over. And I'm here. In a hot spring with a gorgeous guy who could make a girl drool in a thousand different ways.* Melissa takes a few tentative steps out of the water, her skin stinging with the breeze. *Do I dare to climb out and find Dove, exposing myself on the way?*

"Leaving so soon?" he asks. "Here—I'll spill now." He motions for her to follow him in the water, and she goes back in to do so, walking the exaggerated walk of someone in chest-high water. "Check it out."

At the far end of the pool, a narrow inlet leads to an overgrown leafy area where the water is shallower. Melissa feels her top exposed and looks down to see Dove's suit isn't doing her any favors. "Um, you know what, I have to go. I have to meet . . ." She stops in her tracks.

The guy turns to look at her, not flinching when he sees Melissa's hand spread over herself. "Wait. Stay here." He glides by her, going back to the first pool.

Now I scared him for good. Melissa looks up at the moonlight and feels glad at least for the moonlight, the beautiful scenery. "Here you go." He hands her a black T-shirt. "You're obviously weirded out being with me and hey, maybe I don't blame you. But at least you shouldn't have to deal with any bathing suit issues."

Melissa blushes, thankful he can't see it in the dark. "How'd you know?" She slips the T-shirt on and feels much more relaxed.

"Sister. One. She once lost her top at a fancy country club. Another time, she borrowed a suit out of necessity and . . . well, let's just say comedy ensued."

"Thanks," Melissa says and sticks her hand out to shake his. "Now where were you leading me?"

"There." He holds back a palm frond to expose a small waterfall. The forceful water plunges into the pool below, and the guy positions himself directly under the spray of it.

I wish I felt this at ease around everyone, Melissa thinks. *But I'm always learning new things—how to dice onions the way Matty Chase likes them done, how to lead a ski team, how to deal with lost luggage.* "It's remarkably easy to talk to you," Melissa blurts out. She thinks right away that she'll care about looking foolish, but she doesn't.

"Likewise," he says, his voice matter-of-fact. Melissa moves forward into the water, the black T-shirt seeping into the steam, closer to him. At arm's length apart, the spray of the waterfall hits her face. Her heart races again, and this time it has nothing to do with the water's temperature. "Shame we made that pact."

"What pact?" Melissa is entranced by the sound of the water, the feeling of being near him.

"You know," he says, looking away. "Not to do what people do."

"In a situation like this." She completes his sentence.

"Right." He bites his lower lip again.

He has a heart-shaped mouth. Perfect. "Exactly."

They stand next to each other in the spray,

shoulders touching, until they happen to turn toward each other at the same time. Mere inches apart, they could lean in and in a second have their lips meet. Melissa's heart officially pounds, her blood races, her knees tremble despite the warmth of the water.

"Melissa?" A voice from back near the huts interrupts the sultry silence.

Melissa swallows hard and backs away from him, from the waterfall, from everything that almost happened.

"Yeah?" Melissa shouts.

"Van's taking off—leave now or lose your ride." Gus's voice comes through the foliage.

Melissa looks at the guy, her feelings sinking into the steamy water. "I guess I have to go."

He looks at her with his eyebrows raised. "If you're sure about that . . ."

Melissa picks up the hem of the shirt. "Do I need to give this back right now?" *Of course I do*, she thinks. *When else am I going to give it to him? The next random steam-dipping party?* The one thing she is too embarrassed to admit is that she'd seen him before—on the docks—so she can't say she'll give it back to him down there.

He shakes his head. "Nah. Consider it a souvenir." He smiles, still in the shower of the waterfall.

"Of what?" Melissa starts to back away.

"Of a simple, good night. Nothing more, nothing less."

Melissa takes one more look at him and the slightest bit of his orange shorts that she can see as he jumps into the water, and then she leaves.

10

Low tide on the beach brings a vast array of shells. Scattered along the water's edge are conchs, moon snails, and shells that to Dove look like trumpets.

"I can't believe it's happening," she says to Melissa. Dove checks her watch for the hundredth time in an hour. "Ten minutes and he'll be here. After months of waiting." Dove grins. "And I have a whole forty-five minutes with him before I'm due back on the boat for welcome drinks with the owner."

"Sounds like you'll have just enough time to remember why it is you like him!" Melissa gives Dove a hug. "I wish I could stay and watch your heartfelt reunion . . ." She laughs and puts her drawstring bag over her shoulder. Inside, her uniform for work is rolled up and ready to wear. "I'm sure it'll be every bit as romantic as you thought, now that you're both on the same island and William's yacht isn't stuck in the mud."

"So I'll see you back at the docks tonight after work?" Dove looks at Melissa and then into the distance over a small sandy hill for signs of William.

"Not if I can help it," Melissa says, her flip-flops gritty with sand. "I'm hoping today's the last day of waking up feeling seasick." She holds a finger in the air. "Winds of change! I'm finding a place to rent no matter what."

"I'll miss you, but it's probably for the best. If you find a place near the restaurant, you won't have to deal with the bus."

Melissa looks up the hill and sees the brightly colored bus pulling up to the stop. "Speaking of which . . ." She sprints off, leaving Dove to wait for William.

Six minutes. Five minutes. Dove looks out to the water, wondering what she should say to him first. *Is he as nervous as I am? Does he worry about what to talk about?* Dove flashes back, trying to remember great conversations they've had in the past, but stumbles over the memories, mixing them up with more recent talks with Max back in the snow. *We sat by the fire, talking about literature and school and love,* Dove thinks, then feels so much guilt that she blocks the past from her mind and focuses on the sun's bright rays on the water. *He'll be here any minute,* she thinks, and puts her fingertips to her lips. *And then it'll all be fine.*

Up on the hill, the bus pulls over to the white-sand edge of the road and opens its doors. Melissa steps inside and slides into a seat by the window. It's so beautiful here. The waves, the colors of the sand, the sky. She sees Dove in the distance, first just standing still, then jumping up and down and waving. Melissa leans out the open window to see what Dove sees—no doubt William's arrival. At the top of the hill, he stands giving her a double-arm wave, like the kind air traffic controllers use to park planes, both hands above his head. Dove comes running to meet him. He picks her up and she holds on to him with her entire body—legs around his waist, face tucked into his neck. *They're so happy*, Melissa thinks as Dove and William walk toward the bus stop and, presumably, William's car. He's as good-looking as Dove described and somewhat familiar in his broad shoulders and jaunty footing in the sand. Melissa watches William's long, easy strides. As the bus pulls her away from the scene Melissa smiles. It's only when the bus is chugging down the winding road that something occurs to her: She's seen William somewhere before. Somewhere without Dove.

11

"I didn't say massacre the mangoes, I said to puree them," Matty Chase bellows as he blusters his way through the kitchen. Everywhere he goes, criticism and chaos ensue—this dish is too milky, this one's too salty, the ice is melting, the watercress is wilting.

Melissa tries not to feel cowardly, but it's a difficult task when even the most experienced of the staff seem to be getting directions wrong. Everyone, that is, except Melissa. With three large thin metal bowls in front of her, she proceeds with the job at hand: finely slicing green scallions for the first bowl, peeling and chopping purple potatoes and depositing them in iced water, and putting the remainder of the unused food into the third bowl where she can later transport it to the composting center at the end of the beach.

"May I remind you that everything here is green," Matty booms, wiping his wide hands on his apron. "Not as in the color of relaxation, but as in the environmental movement. Very important in this world climate."

The various staff members nod their heads and try to listen to his ranting and raving while working. Melissa picks up a handful of scallions and drops them in the bowl.

"It'll be far more efficient if you pick up the cutting board and dump the whole lot in," Matty says when he's over Melissa's shoulder, surveying her.

Melissa does as he says. "You're right. Don't know why I didn't think of that." She goes back to chopping, distanced by the smell of the scallions and the nagging feeling she's seen William before. *Maybe it's just the photos Dove has,* Melissa thinks, lining the scallions up so she can cut them evenly.

A fellow kitchen worker walks by Melissa's station and bumps her, causing the cutting board to nearly tip onto the floor. "Hey!" Melissa scrambles to fix it.

The girl gives Melissa a fake smile. "Oops."

"No problem," Melissa says, anxious to get back

to work and to avoid problems. "Just watch where you're going."

The girl rolls her eyes. "Look, new girl—"

"Melissa. My name's Melissa."

"Whatever. The point is, just because you've got some secret connection to Matty doesn't give you free rein here."

Melissa is totally caught off guard. "I'm not . . . I don't have any connection to Matty, first of all. And second of all . . ."

"Second of all—" A waiter steps in from the apron station and ties his on crisply. "We all work hard here, Melissa. And we expect the same from you. Right, Olivia?"

"Yeah," Olivia says, her face still set in destroy mode as she watches Melissa. "It's pretty clear Matty has a soft spot for you . . . but the rest of us—well, it's not that easy."

Melissa opens her mouth to protest. "I'm working hard, believe me."

As she's about to explain the pounds of fruit she's cut, the ache in her hands from too much repetitive motion, Matty comes back into the kitchen. "Phone call for you, Melissa."

Melissa looks sheepish as she leaves her station and the smirking Olivia. Matty holds the phone out to Melissa.

"Hello?"

"This is the airport calling with news of your luggage."

Melissa grips the phone, anxious. "Great! Do you have my bags?"

"No, I'm afraid we don't. We continue to apologize for the inconvenience . . ."

"Then why did you call?" Melissa sounds annoyed. From back in the kitchen she can see all the other prep cooks making good use of their time. The waitstaff is nearly ready for the lunch crush.

"It's policy. You left this number and we just wanted to keep you updated. We'll call back with another update soon."

Melissa sighs. "Don't bother."

The heat from the kitchen gets to her and she wipes her forehead with a kitchen towel and goes back to her chopping. *Only three more hours on my feet, chopping, dicing, and prepping, and then I can take a break.*

"It's amazing!" Dove says. "Don't you think it's amazing?" She stares into William's eyes and tries to take it all in. He looks the same, but better. So not the same. Different, but in a good way.

William nods, slipping his warm hand over hers. "I really missed you."

They sit on the wooden bench near the beach parking and watch the cars roll by. Dove thinks about what to say.

"Is this weird?" she asks, her chest rising and falling quickly with each nervous breath.

William doesn't make eye contact but his voice is calm. "A little, don't you think?" He squeezes her hand and turns to face her. "You know what it is? We've just been apart and have to get used to each other. Like muscles."

Dove wrinkles her brow. "What?"

William tries to explain. "Like when you haven't been surfing for a while and then you get back out there, it kind of strains your muscles . . ."

Dove looks disappointed with his metaphor. "Not in a bad way, I hope."

"No, not bad . . . just . . ." William puts his arms around her and hugs her tightly to his chest. "I did miss you, you know."

Dove relishes the feel of his skin on hers, the heat radiating from his face. She pulls back to look at him, their mouths nearly touching. William puts his hands on her cheeks and brings her lips to his. They kiss for what feels to Dove like only seconds, then William pulls away.

"We should go," he says.

Dove catches her breath, still swept up in the haze

of the kissing. "Now?" Just when things are starting to feel normal . . .

"Didn't you say you have to report to work?" William stands up.

Dove's shoulders drop. "Right. Work." *Times like this, I wish I didn't have to work. That I had my nice cushy source of income and didn't have to think about tips and salary and real issues, only this.* She touches William's face, thinking he'll kiss her fingers the way he'd done back at Les Trois, back when they were together every day. But he doesn't. *Doesn't he remember?* Dove wonders. *Are there things I've forgotten?* "I'm already kind of disillusioned with my job, to be honest."

"Oh, yeah?" William waits for her to stand up from the bench.

"It's just . . . don't you ever wish you could do what you want? Not have to deal with the inanities of the daily grind?"

William studies her as if she's said something offensive. "Maybe some of us like work." He sighs.

"What's that supposed to mean?" Dove feels the tension rising between them. *Don't let us fight. It's just an adjustment. Everything's fine. Really.*

"Nothing." William's blond-tipped hair shines in the sun; his broad shoulders tip backward as he goes on. "It's just . . . maybe you aren't cut out for this kind of life."

Dove's eyes are heavy with the seriousness of his voice. "I'm perfectly capable of doing this kind of work," she says. "I can handle the kitchen or galley just as well as, if not better than, many."

William nods. "No, no, I'm not saying you can't. I'm only saying . . . when I'm on the boat, even doing the grunt work, I like it. Maybe when you find what you like, and it's the right fit, it doesn't feel like work." Dove nods, letting his words sink in. "I'll drop you off on my way."

"On your way to where?" Dove asks. "Back to the boat?"

"Nah, into town. One of the guests has requested a certain lotion."

Dove laughs, shaking her head as she and William get into his car. "You really have to get all that for them?"

William nods. "Swab the deck, fix the lines, plot, navigate, charm, and yes, get the lotion."

Dove watches his face as he speaks, feeling the tension melt away between them as they settle into the air-conditioning of the car. *Maybe he's right. Maybe if you're doing what you want to, you don't mind it so much.* Dove tries to think about when she's felt that way, but doesn't have the focus. "So what's so special about this lotion?"

William puts his hand on her thigh and feels her

leg. "It's apparently very moisturizing—or whatever you like to call it. Maybe it smells good. It's overpriced and available only at this one store."

Dove watches the ocean slide by as they head into town. As they pause by the cafés and shops, she watches the ease with which the people on vacation move. *They have nowhere they have to be,* Dove thinks, envying them. *Back at Les Trois, I didn't feel like this. So why now?* She looks at William. "You can drop me here," she says. "It's easier than having to deal with the car gates and locks by the docks."

"Okay," William says. He puts both hands on her shoulders and looks at her long and hard. "It'll be all right."

Dove looks at his eyes, his mouth, the familiar contours of his nose, and the dip above his upper lip. Inside, she feels a trembling building. "Really? Because this all feels . . ." She could cry, but doesn't let herself. *It feels odd. Not like I thought. Why isn't it as simple in reality as it is in my mind?*

"We just have to . . ." William looks out the window. Dove follows his gaze. "That's where I'm headed."

"To Pulse?" Dove asks, looking at the sign.

"Yeah—that's where they sell the lotion."

Dove turns his face to hers and gives him a soft kiss on the lips. "So, wait—what were you saying? About what we need to do?"

William looks out the window, distracted. "Um, right. I guess . . . it feels kind of bizarre right now. With us . . ." He fidgets with his key ring. "But it'll blow over, right?"

Dove makes the decision that the whole reunion feels too heavy, too loaded, too pressured. "We need levity. Fun. You know, to get us back in the swing of things. Remember the summer festival on the mountain?"

"The water slide?" William grins.

"The paddleboat race?" A sweet look overtakes Dove's face as she recalls the day. When was it? She counts back. Over six months ago. More than half a year. Too long.

William nods. "Cool. We'll go out, then. Tonight—if you can get away." He looks toward the front window of Pulse. "I gotta go."

Dove nods, feeling sure that things will improve, that as William said, the muscles of their relationship are just sore from lack of use. "Tonight."

12

Having regained her composure after the phone call, Melissa fills the scallion bowl to the top and brings it to the sous-chef for sautéing.

"You need to compost," Olivia reminds Melissa.

"I know I do," Melissa says, annoyed by Olivia's hawklike gaze.

"Before the lunch crowd gets here—Matty doesn't like them to see us traipsing on the beach with food."

"I'm not going to traipse," Melissa says, and wipes her eyes with her hands, then regrets it. "Ouch. The sting . . ."

Olivia shrugs, watching Melissa's eyes tear up from direct contact with the scallion juice on her fingers. *I hate this job, I hate scallions, I hate the stress.*

"Just have an eye bath," Matty Chase instructs as he breezes by. "Over by the sink—fill up a shot glass with cool water, open your eyes, and tip it back. Works like a charm."

With tears streaming down her cheeks, Melissa heads to the sink and, with her vision blurred, finds a shot glass. "Ugh—it feels terrible."

"Think of something good—you know, a recent calm feeling."

Melissa racks her brain for a feeling like that. "And thinking calm is supposed to help? Everything lately has been so busy—with the flying and the food and working and the . . ."

"You've got to be able to find one perfect, gentle moment . . . At least, that's what my son says." Matty coughs and shakes his head. "Not that my son's the epitome of brilliance and planning at the moment."

Thinking of the warmth of the hot springs, the easy flow of conversation with the boy in the orange shorts, Melissa pats her eyes dry with a clean towel and blinks a few times. Much better. "Tell your son thanks for the advice. It worked."

"Let's hope the same goes for him soon." Matty stirs a long-handled wooden spoon in an oversized pot. "If he had your work ethic, I wouldn't need to find the calm!"

Melissa listens and then collects the food remains and heads to the compost. Outside in the bright light, she squints, tripping on her apron and trying not to spill the scallion ends and potato skins.

She's halfway down the beach when she hears her name. "Melissa!" Olivia shouts, her voice stern even from a distance. "Phone call!"

Melissa feels caught between depositing the compost and heading back for the call. *What if it's my bags and they're all here and I'll have more than three shirts to wear? It's too late to return the clothing and clear the charges to Dove's parents, but it would be nice to at least have my hairbrush . . .*

"Coming!" Melissa trots back up the length of the beach with the full bowl of food ends.

"You're not supposed to get phone calls here," Olivia says, reprimanding her.

"Sorry," Melissa says. *Who made you in charge, anyway?* Sucking up her courage, Melissa asks, "Not to cause problems, but . . . what did I do to offend you?"

Olivia scowls. "It's not just me. It's everyone. You sidestepped the application process, for one. We all had to go through hell to get these jobs. . . ." Olivia pauses, making her hair into a bun so tight it makes her face appear stretched backward. "And besides, we were supposed to have someone else working with us . . ."

Melissa heads toward the phone. "Oh yeah? Who?"

Olivia shrugs. "Never mind—it's over. Just take your phone call and give me the compost. At least one of us has to pull our weight around here." She takes the metal bowl from Melissa's hands and, before Melissa can object, heads out to the beach.

"Look," Melissa says into the phone, "I can't receive calls here, and it's hard to believe my bags magically showed up, so . . ."

A voice comes through the receiver. "What the hell are you talking about? I don't have your bags."

"Harley?" Melissa smiles, then groans. "Don't call me here. It's not allowed . . ."

"I know—remember? But I couldn't resist."

Melissa watches the annoyed faces of the staff and whispers, "I'm kind of on everyone's shit list here. And for no good reason."

"Ohhh," Harley teases, "you must be Matty Chase's favorite. Everyone always has it in for the one who doesn't have to work as hard."

Melissa picks at a spot on her side. "That's not true. I work just as hard. They're just . . . I don't even know."

Harley speaks quickly. "Look, just stay extra-late tonight. Skip the party I was going to tell you about—"

"But I . . ."

"No buts. Listen, I'll go to this party solo . . . or not so solo, as the case may be." Harley's grin is nearly audible. "And then we'll meet tomorrow at Lemon Quay Beach to catch up."

"Lemon Quay?"

"It's private, but I know someone . . ."

"You always know someone," Melissa says, feeling the need to get back to work.

"I grew up in a restaurant. Granted, it was a dive and nothing like Matty Chase's empire, but my advice is . . . stay late tonight and make all your hard work show. Your problem is that you make it look too easy. I know that's your thing, but it comes off as too slick. Which is probably why Matty likes you."

"Thanks for the input, Harley," Melissa says. "I'll see you tomorrow." She's about to hang up when she remembers something. "Hey, Harley?"

"Yeah?"

"Aren't you going to tell me who the guy is?"

Harley's deep laugh invades the phone. "Let me just see how tonight goes and I'll get back to you." She pauses. "Say hi to Dove for me."

"I will," Melissa says, looking at the giant wipeable board that displays everyone's tasks. "But if I can possibly manage it, I won't see her until tomorrow at least—if I can find somewhere else to stay."

"Good luck," Harley says.

Under Melissa's name on the board is *Smoothie bar*. "I might need it," Melissa says. *At least I'll get to be outside,* she thinks. *Not that I've ever made a smoothie in my life. But how complicated can it be?*

Many ticking hours later, after serving green tea mango smoothies with a twist, the naked peach (which, to her humiliation, Melissa found out wasn't "naked" but "ma-ked," a type of local produce, lots of chocolate swirls and coffee berries, and every kind of concoction in between), Melissa is ready to go home.

"Only, I don't exactly have a home," she explains to Olivia. Melissa wearily wipes the smoothie bar down yet again and fills an order for a strawberry guava mousse with lime. "And if I have to spend another night on the yacht I will just scream."

"Yeah, life on a luxury yacht," Olivia says sarcastically. "Sounds rough."

"I get seasick."

"So? You work here—and we're basically at sea," she says. Over the course of the day Melissa has seen Olivia ease up just a tad, particularly after Melissa agreed to pull a double shift, as per Harley's suggestion, and work the smoothie bar in the evening when the beach-going crowd fills every outside seat.

"I just need to have a place to sleep that doesn't move." Melissa swiftly hands over two more drinks to servers while Olivia prepares two glasses by rolling their rims in crushed ice and sugar.

Olivia watches Melissa's determination as she works. "Well, I'm already crashing with friends, but if I hear of anything, I'll let you know."

Melissa gives Olivia a real smile. *It's not much, but it's something,* Melissa thinks. *She might not like me, but maybe she won't actively hate me.* She studies the crowd of people waiting for their drinks.

A woman in a bright turquoise top waves. "Hello! Over here!"

"You know her?" Olivia asks, caught between disbelief and disapproval.

Melissa nods reluctantly. "Kind of. She's a friend of a friend. Hi, Emmy!"

Emmy Taylor approaches the smoothie bar, jostling a waiter out of the way so she can talk to Melissa. "How quaint—you work here?"

Melissa nods. "Here's the cappuccino delight. Table eight. No, six."

Olivia goes back to smirking as Melissa tries to balance her work and listening to Emmy rant and rave.

"So, there we were, all of us at the hot springs—you really should go sometime, Melissa, it's so fun." Emmy's blue eyes are wide with excitement.

"So I hear," says Melissa, recalling for the second time today the relaxing feeling of being immersed in water. *Was it the water or the company?* she wonders.

"And to make a long story short, I'm having a party next Saturday . . ." She leans in, making sure to keep her voice loud enough to inspire eavesdropping. "It'll be the event of the season. Literally. It's being covered by all the entertainment news shows—and featured in magazines." She rolls her eyes good-naturedly. "It's not my doing—just some press thing my parents put together. But you should come. And bring Dove, of course."

"You told us." Melissa keeps working but nods. "Sounds . . . fun."

"It will be. It's at the Botanical Gardens," Emmy says. She stares while Melissa wipes up a blotch of melted chocolate. "Sorry you have to work, or you could join us."

Melissa straightens herself up. "You don't have to be sorry," she says, really feeling it. *So what if I've worked all day and still have six hours to go?* "I like it, actually."

"Must be the right job for you, then," Emmy says. "I have to get back to my table, but come say hi if you get a sec."

Melissa watches Emmy glide back to her table and sit down with a cluster of friends.

Skeptical, Olivia asks, “You sure you don’t know them?”

“I don’t,” Melissa says, looking at Emmy’s table, at her tanned and poised friends. Across from her, with his chair slightly askew, is Max. “Well, maybe I semi-know one of them.” As if on cue, Max looks up from his blended drink, looks at Melissa, and gives a nod.

The Sugar Hut, Melissa thinks. *That’s where Max is staying. It’s got tons of rooms. Would it be so bad if I asked him for one night’s accommodation?* Melissa wipes her cold hands on a towel and looks again at Max, who offers up his kind smile. “Hey, Olivia, can you make an island mint cream? I’ll be right back. Promise.”

13

"Are you here with anyone?" Dove asks Harley. Her words rush out in a burst of energy. The friends have said their hellos and hugged and gotten past any residual feelings of resentment left over from their time at Les Trois. *In my worst nightmare*, Dove thinks, *I pictured finding Harley slathering sunblock on William.* She smiles at Harley, glad her friend is alone—at least for the time being.

Dove wears a halter dress in the palest shade of blue, highlighting her eyes, and simple sandals. The night air is warm with just a slight breeze. "It's so funny to see you without boots and a heavy jacket."

"I know, right?" Harley reties the shoulder strap of her dress. *So maybe I borrowed a few items from the store to wear for special occasions—no big deal, right?* She looks down at the palm print dress and remembers the compliment she got for it. "I am here with someone." She grins. "A him."

Dove looks around for evidence of this someone. "Really?"

Harley nods. "He just went off to find me something to eat. I was so busy at Pulse today I forgot to have lunch. As a result, I'm about to fall over." Harley fakes passing out.

"I know Pulse," Dove says, thinking back to her carefree charge account days. Dove remembers that William went to Pulse today but feels strange bringing him up, like the mere mention of his name will jinx the good feeling she has. *I don't want Harley to think I'm checking up on him or not trusting her. Besides, she looks so happy.* "You seem in great shape. Obviously, the island agrees with you."

"Definitely," Harley affirms.

"It's so funny," Dove says, blushing as she admits this, "I was paranoid that you and William would . . ." She shakes her head. "You know . . ."

Harley looks at Dove like she's bonkers. "No way. I may be a lot of things, but I'm not actively out to get your boyfriend." Harley's thick hair sweeps against her shoulders, making her look dramatic and beautiful. "Besides, I heard you drone on and on about him back at the chalet. I hardly think he'd be my type."

Dove grins, ogling Harley's hair and wishing yet again that she hadn't chopped hers off in a fit of illogical emotions. "You're right. And I'm sorry for even thinking it." She pauses, fiddling with her bracelet. It's a thin piece of string worn down to nearly nothing that she'd found on a hike with William way back in the summer. He'd tied it on her wrist as they sat watching the birds swoop over the green grass and she never thought she'd keep it on so long, but now it was like a talisman and she couldn't get rid of it. "So . . . what's his name?"

Harley opens her mouth to speak but then bolts. Looking back over her shoulder, her dress billowing in a gust of wind, she explains, "I can see my guy—and my food. Catch you later!"

Dove stands on her tiptoes to see Harley's friend but can't see anyone. *Maybe she's making him up. No, that's mean of me. Why would she do that? I'm sure she snagged some hot college guy on break or something. But what's his name?* She waits for William to return to the stone patio where couples dance and talk, and a rowdy conga line takes shape, then disperses as people laugh and play games. *Yeah, Harley probably wooed some college boy who couldn't stop staring at her legs.*

College. The word sends shivers down Dove's bare back. *What if I never go? Will it matter?* She thinks about her talks with Max and his Oxford teacher, Professor Hartman, who encouraged Dove's intellect. Talking to Max about going to Oxford had been easy, but Dove knows if she brought up the subject with William, they'd have to deal with more than just what was right for Dove. They'd have to deal with their future as a couple.

"So . . . I got you something," William says, creeping up to Dove from behind.

Dove shivers again, this time from the proximity to William. Their kiss by the ocean only reminded her of other kisses and how great they could feel. William snakes his hands around Dove's waist, then puts something on her neck.

"When we were grounded on St. Kitts, I picked this up." He clasps a tube-shaped sterling-silver pendant around her neck.

"It's beautiful," she says, beaming. The music from the party blares on, but she feels oblivious to the noise, to the crowds.

"It's filled with something," William explains.

"Should I open it?" Dove asks, her fingers poised to do so.

"No!" William stops her. "There's . . . it's an old island legend. You buy two of these and in one you write your feelings and in the other you collect this famous sand."

"Sand can be famous?" Dove makes him laugh.

"I guess. Anyway, at Dieppe Bay there's all this pure black sand."

"So, true love in one container, black sand in the other?" Dove looks confused.

"Yeah. Exactly. And you're supposed to keep one and give the other one away." He kisses the back of Dove's neck and spins her around to the music. They sway close together for a minute. "And, as legend goes, when the time is right, you open the thing up and if it's black sand, it's over." He casually swats at the air. Then he pulls her in very tightly. "And if you have true love, the note will appear and . . ."

"The rest is history?" Dove dances with him, so happy to be in his arms.

"Right." The music ends. "You thirsty?" Dove nods. "I'll get us some drinks—they've got a major daiquiri bar going."

"No alcohol in mine," she reminds him. "I have early call at five a.m."

Dove stands there, touching her new necklace and waiting for William to come back. *If I opened it, what would I find? True love or black sand?* She lets the pendant grace her neck but does not open it to find out.

"Again, thanks so much for having me," Melissa says. The burnished brass clock on her bedside table reads two o'clock. She yawns, thoroughly exhausted after pulling not only a double shift and a grueling stint at the smoothie bar, but—to further ingratiate herself with Olivia and the others—a massive cleanup of the stockroom, cold storage, and freezer. Her hands are still slightly blue from the cold. "I know we're not exactly friends, but again, I do appreciate the help."

Max goes to the closet and hands Melissa two fluffy towels, a brand-new toothbrush, and shampoo. "Believe me, no one will notice you're here—the place is way too big for anyone's good." He watches her look around. The room has a king-sized bed, sitting area, en suite bathroom with whirlpool and steam shower, and glass windows overlooking the water.

"It's amazing is what it is." Melissa sighs. "If I weren't so tired, I'd be jumping around."

Max nods. "It's lovely. It's fine."

Melissa notes that Max's usual charm, the wit and snarky behavior, seem to be lacking. "Are you okay, Max? You seem . . ."

Max doesn't wait for a more probing question. He launches into a tirade, lounging on the chaise in the sitting area while Melissa perches on the bed.

"It's just—she's so frustrating! Or maybe I'm stupid and to blame for the entire mess to begin with. It depends how far back you go."

"Sorry?" Melissa waits for Max to explain. *I can't believe how exhausted I am. Too tired to remove my shoes. Too tired to have to get up in a few hours to meet Harley and hear about her recent exploits with her nameless beau. And just what is his name, anyway?* Melissa makes a mental note to demand that Harley reveal his name. The anvil-heavy weight of her body makes Melissa sink further into the bed. *I'm too tired for anything.*

Max doesn't notice the circles under Melissa's eyes, the droop of her mouth. He lies down as though talking to a therapist, his hands gesturing, his mind whirring. "Here's the thing, okay?" He blushes for one second, then regains a businesslike composure. "I'm in love with Dove. Totally and completely. And—before you can say it—her old friend Claire, who showed up at Les Trois, had nothing to do with me. Or rather, I had nothing to do with her. I haven't had anything to do with anyone, romantically speaking, since I realized I love Dove."

Melissa lies down on her stomach on the bed, feeling that this conversation might take a while. She frees her hair from its restaurant-tight elastic. "And when was that, exactly?"

Max turns his head to face her. "Since last spring."

"Last spring? Jeez—that was before Dove even came to Les Trois. Before she . . ." Melissa stops herself. *God, this guy has it bad. Why is it I have no guys falling at my feet and Dove has too many to deal with?*

"I know, I know. Before she met the guy whose name shall not be mentioned."

"William?"

Max groans. "Ugh—you mentioned his name. But yeah, that's what I keep annoying myself with—I mean, if I'd only spoken up then, gone to see her in London right after we graduated but before she left for the summer . . ."

Melissa shakes her head, her curls springing. "You can't change what's in the past, Max."

"I know, I know. I just wish that she'd see the light."

Melissa longs so much for bed but she can't cut Max off—he did offer her a place to stay, after all. "What light is that, exactly?"

"Me," Max says. "I'm the light."

Maybe Dove's got it wrong, Melissa thinks. *If she could only hear Max's plea, or if Max didn't suddenly get all dramatic in front of her. But no, she's got William and that's who she wants . . .*

Melissa stares at the clock, willing it to be earlier

so she can get more sleep before meeting Harley at the beach. "Wait," she says, remembering something.

"What's wrong?"

"Nothing," Melissa says, counting on her fingers, her mind playing mental calendar. "It's just easy to lose track of the days and dates here."

"I know what you mean." Max nods, his gorgeous face registering only signs of defeat. "My hopes were so far up coming here, and now every day just sort of slides into the next."

Melissa yawns. She'd like nothing more than to slide under the sheets and forget about her long day, leave behind her romantic woes and the pining for people like the guy in the orange shorts or Gabe way off in some Nordic country. "I'm so tired," Melissa says aloud, hoping Max will get the hint. *I just want to go to bed and forget. Forget about my aching hands and feet and heart and forget about the as-yet-untold significance of tomorrow.*

"I'm tired, too," Max says but he doesn't budge. "Tired of liking and liking and having my feelings hit a wall."

Melissa nods. *At least I can relate*, she thinks and settles in for what she's sure will be hours of listening to Max.

14

"How come you seem blah today?" Harley asks, her head throbbing from too much sun and spiked punch the night before. "And hey, remind me later on, just in case I'm tempted, not to drink anything with alcohol. Last night, consuming too much, not good." She holds her head in her hands.

"Sure. Whatever you say," Melissa agrees. She puts her fingers to her nose, smelling yet again the sharpness of twenty pounds of sliced onions. Having been up almost the whole night, she went in to help with early-morning prep before meeting Harley. Using the mandoline food grater was no help in terms of stench. "Just call me Onion Girl." Melissa's eyes drift away from the conversation and out toward the water's edge.

Harley turns to lie on her stomach, untying her magenta bikini top as she goes, but lying flat quickly to avoid exposing too much. "Really, Mel, you seem weird today."

Melissa shrugs. "It's nothing."

"Nothing meaning really nada or nothing meaning you're pissed at me and not telling me or upset about work and not expressing it or . . ."

Melissa stares out at the familiar blue of the water. *How peaceful to be floating on my back out there.* "I remember swimming when I was a kid, how nothing mattered in the world on land. Just being in the water was fun enough." She closes her eyes, feeling the sun's harsh rays on her face, illuminating behind her eyelids so she feels as though she's seeing peach-colored air. "Now it's like everything on land is what's most important."

Harley motions for Melissa to tie her top for her and Melissa obliges. Harley then sits up abruptly, studying Melissa's face. "Are you having a massive existential crisis?"

Melissa cracks a smile. She sits next to Harley and trails her fingers in the hot sand, sprinkling some on her legs. "Sometimes it's like I watch you and Dove and I feel like I'm never going to have that."

"That what?" Harley's chestnut hair swings over her shoulders, her lips the color of ripe plums.

"That!" Melissa points to a couple of guys walking by who have their eyes pinned to Harley's visage.

Harley hardly gives them a glance as she adjusts her top. When her hands reach her neck, she pauses. "Oh, no! Crap."

"What?" Melissa asks.

Harley continues to feel her neck and then looks on the sand. "I lost something. I think." She waits, thinking. "Or maybe I left it somewhere, which isn't really the same thing as losing it. Never mind. Crisis averted."

Melissa sighs. "Okay . . ."

Harley goes back to Melissa. "Don't get down on yourself. . . . You have plenty of appeal." She pauses. "Remember Gabe? And James? I seem to recall they preferred your je ne sais quoi to . . ." She laughs, and adds jokingly, "To my fine figure. Granted, they never saw this bathing suit." She laughs at herself.

Melissa winces upon hearing Gabe's name. Days and distance haven't dulled the feeling of missing him. *But then, how can you miss what you never really had?* she wonders, touching the apples of her cheeks. "I'm going to burn if I don't get inside or in the shade soon. Besides, I have about fifteen pounds of guava to chop."

"Making daiquiris?" Harley asks, frowning.

"No—and no drinking for you, remember? I have to make salsa—tropical salsa. Thus the onions. Olivia's in charge of the pineapples."

"Sounds like you're on Matty Chase's good side. A great place to be. Most people when they start out have to haul trash or fish heads."

"I guess I'd choose guava," Melissa says. Then she remembers her mental note from the previous night. "Hey, you know what? You have to tell me his name."

"Whose name?"

"Don't play dumb with me, Harley. Just get out with it." Melissa mimes looking at her watch, tapping her foot in the sand as though she's in a hurry. *I could be in a hurry,* she thinks, *if I wanted to get to the restaurant early and get in some good face time with Matty Chase. I'm on his good side, sure, but it couldn't hurt to be even better.* Melissa doesn't let herself think about what she really hopes: that Matthew Chase—*the* Matthew Chase—might offer her a job at one of his other restaurants. *I could travel the world if I got accepted into his enterprise.* "While I'm waiting for your answer, can I tell you what I read on the plane? That in-flight magazine had photos of Matty Chase's dining establishments, the new spa he's opening up in California. . . . Anyway, so many of the people who've worked with him end up doing cool stuff. Writing cookbooks, starting their own restaurants . . ."

"Getting television shows—like his son . . ." Harley adds. She reaches into her bag and grabs a tube of sunblock. After she slides cream onto her arms and shoulders, she tilts her head. "So . . . you really want to know?"

"The name of your latest crush?"

"He's not a crush. He's it," Harley says definitively.

"Yes, please." Melissa takes the sunblock and dabs some on her face, neglecting to rub it in on her nose.

"His name is . . ." A huge grin spreads over Harley's chiseled face. "Bug."

"Bug?" Melissa stands with her eyebrows raised, still not rubbing in the sunblock.

"I know, I know. You thought it'd be something cool like Drake or Dylan or whatever. But Bug's his name."

"His nickname, you mean?"

Harley shrugs. "I sort of assumed he was like one of those models or singers—the ones with only a first name." She strikes a pose and pretends that she's being photographed. "Doesn't bother me."

Melissa returns Harley's grin. "Sounds—fun."

Harley gets so distracted by thoughts of her love's name that she doesn't tell Melissa about the blob of white cream on her nose, either.

"He *is* fun. Fun and fantastic!" Harley nods and

stands up, stretching her bikinied self and causing more than a little commotion from nearby groups of guys. "Just tell me one thing before you leave me beached by myself."

Not for long, I bet, Melissa thinks but doesn't say. *Bug will show up with some entourage of cool people, all in couples. It's not like I'm bitter—more like I'm feeling sorry for myself.* "Well, I look forward to meeting this insect of yours."

"Bug."

"Spider, insect, bug, animal, vegetable, mineral."

"Hot mineral," Harley chides.

Melissa prepares to leave, readying herself for hours with pounds of guava as her only companion. Far off by the covered beach bar, she sees a pair of bright orange shorts. She squints, trying to see if they belong to the guy she saw at the docks, the same one who appeared at the hot springs. The same one she couldn't shake off from her dreams.

I need to give him a name. But what to call him? Beach Boy? Hot Springs Hottie? No—Orange Shorts. And oh man, it is him! I could swear he sees me, Melissa thinks, blushing and burning. *If I weren't so worried about being humiliated, I'd ask him right now. But what if he doesn't even remember being with me at the hot springs? Or worse, remembers it and wishes he didn't.*

"I have to go, Harl." Melissa watches Orange

Shorts walk closer. *He's definitely seen me staring at him. Great. Now I'll be Onion Girl and Stalker Girl.* "Seriously, I'll see you after work. I'm only on prep and since I went in early to . . ."

"Kiss ass . . ." Harley fills in.

"No . . . okay, sort of . . . anyway, I have salsa and then I'm done. Around six."

"Well, let me check with Bug and figure out a plan for later. We'll get you out of this fog."

Melissa starts off down the beach, lifting her feet as she goes so they won't sting on the hot sand.

"Wait!" Melissa halts in her tracks. "You never answered me!" Harley yells to her.

"You never really asked me anything!" Melissa laughs, her curls bobbing as she giggles. Harley might be a beach goddess but at least she has a good head on her shoulders.

"What, in fact, is the giant chip on your shoulder because of?"

"Nice grammar!" Melissa yells.

Harley runs over, pouting. "Fine. Make fun of my lack of schooling. I might not have Dove's elocution or your worldly ways, but who else has been so invested in your woes?"

"True." Melissa sighs, wondering whether to spill the proverbial beans or not. *This day was bound to be weird.*

"Is this boy related?"

Melissa checks over her shoulder for Orange Shorts and feels both relieved and saddened when she can't see him anymore. "No. Not really."

Harley kicks sand at her friend. "Out with it, then."

"Okay." Melissa takes a deep breath. "If you want to know the real reason for my blahs today . . ." She pauses. Suddenly, as close as a few beach-spread towels away, Orange Shorts is there. And not only there, but giving her a look that tells her he does know who she is. But does he *want* to know? Melissa feels her blood zooming around her veins and senses the need to vacate the scene as soon as possible. "I, uh, ummm . . ."

Harley rolls her eyes. "Are you a spy or something?" she asks too loud.

Orange Shorts and a couple of other people hear and laugh. Melissa feels her face for further signs of burning or blushing and then realizes she has the sunblock blob attached to her nose. *Nice work. No wonder Orange Shorts is laughing.* "No. I'm not secret service or MI5 . . . I'm . . . it's . . ."

Harley pivots, crossing her arms over her chest defensively. "Never mind. Forget I asked. Clearly you don't trust me to—"

"It's my birthday," Melissa says softly.

"What?" Harley yelps, turning back toward her, leaning in closer.

"It's my birthday," Melissa says again in a regular voice.

"Wait—sorry. One more time?" Harley puts her hands on her hips.

Melissa grins, yelling, "It's my birthday!!"

Orange Shorts and his friends clap, causing a true blush to seep over Melissa's face.

Harley looks smug and pats Melissa on the head. "Well, why didn't you say something sooner?" She thinks for a second as Melissa glances at Orange Shorts, regrets doing so, and prepares to bolt. "I'll pick you up at the restaurant at six sharp. That should give us time to run back to Pulse and change."

Melissa backs away. "Okay—but why?"

"Don't you worry your pretty little head about it. Just enjoy the next few birthday hours. Maybe Matty Chase'll give you a free dessert or something in honor of your special day."

"Maybe he'll offer me top pick of any job at any of his restaurants worldwide."

"Maybe you're dreaming!" Harley yells.

Melissa nods at her, glad to have her secret off her chest even if it didn't exactly result in a parade or balloons being magically delivered in her honor.

"I'll see you later, Harley." Melissa waves, trying

still to ignore Orange Shorts. *Maybe I won't like him or recognize him if he wears something else.* Silently, she wills him to change into acid-wash jeans or a polyester leisure suit—anything to make her not focus on him.

"And, Mel? Try not to reek of onions when I get you, okay?"

Melissa, far away enough from Orange Shorts and the slight embarrassment of being on public birthday display to feel her pulse slow, cups her hands in front of her like a megaphone. "No onions for me, no daiquiris for you, and maybe a piece of cake for both of us?"

Harley nods. "You bet. Cake on me."

15

"I'm sorry," Dove says, her voice soft not because she wants to appear cowardly but because she's embarrassed.

"Well, sorry's not going to cut it," Gus says. "Did you see their faces? You dropped the entire tray of appetizers. Not one, not two, but the whole thing."

Dove snaps. "No kidding. I was there. I was the one who spent my entire day prepping the food, remember?" Dove flashes back to rolling out the pastry dough so it was thin enough to see through, then spreading layers of Camembert cheese and roasted island vegetables inside. "Labor-intensive work with no payoff. Not exactly what I signed up for." She sighs.

Gus stares at her. "Well, the owner's not happy. I can tell you that. They've gone out to dinner now, but you should know you're on probation."

Shock rattles through Dove's body. "Probation? I'm in culinary jail?"

"Not jail, just—"

"Just nothing. God, all I did was spill a tray. It's no catastrophe." Dove finishes putting away the utensils in their small drawer and then latches the cooler closed for the evening.

"Look, I told you right off—there's no room for mistakes." Gus's voice softens. "You won't be fired. Not yet, anyway. Just show her tomorrow at breakfast. Wow her with your abilities and it'll all be fine."

Dove purses her lips and looks down at the galley floor. "I have to mop." *Then I have to mope*, she thinks. *Remind me again how I got into this mess?* She puts on her best fake upbeat voice. "But I'll make sure to whip up a wonderful breakfast."

Gus grins, oblivious to her sarcasm. "Great."

At the dockside rotunda Harley sits in her shorts and tank top, her bare feet resting on the rungs of the stool, with a box of Mylar balloons to her left and a tank of helium to her right. On autopilot, she takes balloon after balloon and fills it, ties it closed, then secures a matching red, yellow, or green ribbon to its bottom.

This is just what Melissa needs, she thinks, looking at the bunches of floating balloons. *She's so ready for a pick-me-up. It's hard to be the one left out—with Dove and William and me and Bug, maybe Melissa feels like the perpetual third wheel. But I'll make it better for her.* Harley smiles to herself, feeling content amid the shining foil, the calm ocean breezes, and the feelings of love she has brewing inside. *Bug. Who'd have thought I'd come to some random island and find Mr. Right? The world always turns out in different ways than you think it will, and tonight will be no exception. Parties always have the potential to throw a few surprises—that's what makes them fun. Melissa could meet the guy of her dreams tonight. Or just have a fun time and forget her job stressors.*

Harley pictures dancing with Bug, his blond-tipped hair brushing gently against her face, his arms encircling her. *What had he said to her this afternoon when he stopped by, surprising her with the jewelry she'd lost on the beach with Melissa? "When it's right, it's right and you know it with every part of your body and brain," he'd whispered into her ear.* That's what keeps echoing in Harley's mind as she finishes inflating the last of the balloons and checks her watch.

The preparations are set, the tent, the music, food

being catered by the Seafood Shanty down the beach, her outfit coming courtesy of a tiny false charge at Pulse. *Dove won't mind*, Harley thinks when she slips into her muted orange flowy dress. *Besides, Melissa charged her stuff, and I did mine with my staff discount*. Harley takes one last look at the setup, securing the balloons to each pole of the rotunda tent. The party will be a vision of red, green, and yellow. *Time to head out to pick up the birthday girl.*

"The only good thing about not having my clothing back from the land of lost luggage is that I don't have to spend time wondering what to wear," Melissa says as she shimmies into her one dress and attempts to zip it up herself. The mirror in the guest room at Max's house stretches out wall-length.

"Hey, Birthday Girl," Max says, his words following a swift knock on the door.

"Who told you?" Melissa inquires, fixing a twisted shoulder strap and wishing she'd had the guts to charge a pair of shoes. Looks like it's flip-flops yet again. She slips into them, wondering if her luggage will ever arrive. "By the time my bags get to this island, it'll be time to . . ." Her voice trails off. Time to what, exactly? Not like I have some grand plan beyond living in the moment.

Max watches Melissa study her reflection. "Let's just say word spreads quickly. And Harley has a rather big mouth."

"Yeah, but it's always blabbing about fun stuff."

Max nods. In his white shirt and baggy khaki trousers he is every inch the classic good-looking brooder. "So, it's okay if I tag along tonight?"

"Sure," Melissa says, then reiterates, "It's not like I planned this. Any of this . . ." She knows she's referring to more than just the party tonight. "You know, all along I kept thinking I had it all sorted out—work at the chalets, have fun, and the rest would just come to me."

Max hoists himself up on the wide window ledge, one leg swung out onto the balcony, the other safely inside. "And that's not the case?"

Melissa shrugs. "Well, obviously, I swerved off whatever path I was on. No more chalet."

"But you like your new job, right?"

"I do." She furrows her brow. "A lot, actually. Despite the fact that they sent me home early today for no good reason."

"Maybe Matty Chase got wind of your impending celebration," Max suggests with a laugh.

"Doubtful. He's more inclined to keep people at work for the entire duration of their birthdays, isn't he? At least that's what I hear."

Max gives her a goofy look. "Oh, but he has a soft spot for sweet Melissa Forsythe."

Melissa gives her best ingenue face. "Yes, folks, that's right, I am the teacher's pet." She flashes back to school, to being in class, and then to finishing school and starting the next phase of life. "Yeah, I really like my job, but . . ." Tugging at her curls, Melissa tests out how she would look with straight hair, pulling it taut. As soon as she releases the hair it springs back into tight coils. She shakes her head.

"What comes next? Ah, isn't that the big question?" Max glances out toward the water. The sun has begun its descent, sending rays of various shades of yellow and pink onto the ocean's surface.

"You have it all figured out, don't you, Max?"

Max stands up. "Oh, sure. Go back to Oxford, study for a few more years, finish with high honors, write the next brilliant novel, get wildly famous and become . . ." He shakes his head, causing his dark hair to flop into his green eyes.

Melissa sidles up next to him. The festive mood of the evening begins to swirl around her, making her wonder what might happen. *Maybe I'll see Orange Shorts, maybe I'll find my luggage, maybe I'll just end up having a decent birthday rather than keeping it tucked way inside.* "Maybe that's my problem!" she says aloud. "Just like I kept this day—this one day a year you're supposed to celebrate yourself—a secret. . . . Maybe you're supposed to just say it."

"Huh?" Max looks at her like she's lost it.

Melissa pokes Max's chest. "You. You want to write a novel, correct? And let me guess what it'll be about. Some unrequited love story—a bookish, brooding boy loves this girl. And despite numerous attempts to convince her, he never does that one big grand gesture that really tells her how he feels. The end."

Max coughs and sighs at the same time. "So you're saying I should tell her yet again?"

Melissa stares at her flip-flops. "As many times as I've worn these things is how many times you have to repeat it to Dove. Yes, Max, tell Dove how you feel. Not with a question of should you stay or go, not with any kind of question at all."

"A definitive declaration?" Max ambles to the doorway, gesturing with his hand for Melissa to lead the way down the grand staircase toward the car.

"Yes. You tell her how you feel and I . . ."

"You'll?" Max holds the heavy double wooden door open for Melissa and she steps out into the breezy evening. Wind sweeps up through the palm fronds, sending a ruffling noise down toward her. She shivers.

"I'll . . . I don't know," she says. "But I'm determined to find out."

In a space that resembles a cave more than a bed, Dove tries to get comfortable. Propped up behind her is the one thin pillow she's been given on board the yacht. To bolster it, she rolls up a sweatshirt, a towel, and a pair of pants, but still manages to sink back.

"Ahhh," she groans aloud, annoyed that she can't be above in the sitting areas because the owner is there and she can't be in the galley lest she be ordered to make more food even though she's technically off duty. "I can't go anywhere."

Footsteps on the ladder that leads down into the crew's quarters produce a smiling William. "Why go anywhere when you can have there brought to you?"

Dove puts her textbook down and sits up fast, clunking her head on the low ceiling of the bunk above her. "Ow."

"Good to see you, too." William presents her with a kiss on the cheek and crouches down so he can sit near her on the edge of the bunk.

"Slide in," Dove suggests, patting the space next to her.

William obliges, stretching his lanky frame out over the length of the bunk. He grimaces and turns on his side. "What is this? It's digging into me."

"A book."

William gives her a look. "Um, yeah, I can see that. I can feel it, too."

Dove takes the heavy text from his hands and shelves it with her rolled-up socks in a small space at the foot of the bunk. "Just pleasure reading."

"Looks more like schoolwork."

Dove shrugs. "I guess it could be. For some. Sorry it came between us . . ." she jokes and lies down so the left side of her body overlaps his.

"Yup, that's right. Academics gets between us every time." He means it as a joke, but it comes out heavier than intended.

Dove worries he means something by it and tries to smooth over the awkwardness with kisses. A tiny part of her knows she and William really are very different—she'd gone to the best schools and he hadn't—but more than this, he didn't seem to care about the future. *And do I? Sure, it's possible to be with someone whose past isn't like yours, but what if your futures don't match up either?*

Dove bites her lip, frowning, and then tries to shake off the whole ordeal with more kisses. She kisses his arms, then his shoulder, then his neck, then his chin. As she kisses his face, her necklace bumps into his cheek.

"Wait—this thing is . . ." William tugs on her necklace. "Can't you take it off?"

"You have me alone in the crew's quarters and you want to remove my . . . necklace?" Dove laughs. She touches the silver chain and shakes her head. "I don't want to."

William looks annoyed and then softens. "You like it that much? It's just a—"

"It's just a meaningful gift, is what it is." Dove lies flat on her back next to William and takes his hand in hers. "I'm glad you came by. I was beginning to loathe this evening." Dove thinks about her run-in with Gus, how she'll have to wow everyone at breakfast, how when she thought about being on the island with William, it wasn't like this. He squeezes her hand. Well, maybe it was like this part . . .

"Hey." William puts his hand on his head, propping himself up so he can look down at Dove. "You up for coming out tonight?"

Dove's spirits flag. "Tonight? Didn't I just say I was tired?"

"No, you said you were starting to loathe this night. Different story."

"Well, I amend my previous comment. I had a long day; I'm all set for an even longer morning, and—no. I don't really want to go out." She stares at him, flashing her sweet smile, batting her eyes and pulling him down for a kiss.

William puts his lips on hers, their mouths meeting with an intense kiss that goes on and on until Dove is breathless.

"Whoa." William pauses.

Dove looks deep into his eyes, searching for signs he feels as she does, wrapped up in the moment and keen to keep the kiss and anything else that follows going. "Here," she says and tugs at his shirt.

William grins but then pulls back. "Hey—let's go out. It'll be fun."

Dove feels the pit in her stomach that started as passion widen to disappointment. "You're saying you want to leave our cozy little world and go up there?" She points up the ladder to whatever is waiting in the world above.

William scratches his head, avoiding eye contact. "I just think it's good for us to be social, you know?"

Dove nods, trying to agree with him, but finding that she still wants to stay. "You go. I've got reading to do." He starts to object. "Really, it's fine. We'll meet up tomorrow. Wait. Not tomorrow. I've got a crazy day. The next day."

William shakes his head. "We've been chartered for a day trip to the casinos."

Dove frowns. "The weekend?"

William nods, considering the options, heavy into his thoughts. "I guess . . ."

Dove tries to rally, to perk things up. "I know it's not what we pictured, all this work coming between us."

William points to her reading material. "And textbooks . . ." He smiles.

"But . . ." She thinks about how William always likes a good party, a reason for being festive. Not that she doesn't, but she's more inclined for a quiet night where he's more into a limbo on the beach or a grand soiree. "An old friend, Emmy Taylor—she's having some giant bash at the—"

"Botanical Gardens?" William's eyes light up. "I totally want to go to that. Sounds like the event of the season. I didn't know you know her."

Dove wrinkles her forehead. "Do you?"

William shrugs. "Only in the way that most people cross paths at some point or another here. But yeah, cool, I'm game for that." He leans in and hugs Dove.

"So I'll see you then?" Dove feels let down, but not devastated. *It's better this way*, she decides. *He can go have fun being social and I can get my rest. Then we'll have a romantic and social and meaningful night at the Botanical Gardens. And I won't be the girl who held him back and he won't be the guy who dragged me away from work.*

"I'll see you." William nods as he plants a quick kiss on her lips and climbs the ladder.

A few minutes later, steps on the ladder make Dove's pulse race. *He came back! He doesn't want to be social without me. Besides, I should go out with him.* Dove puts her book away again and rises from the bunk, readying to go.

"Hey!" Melissa says from the ladder.

Dove turns toward her, surprised. "Oh, hi."

"Don't sound so excited to see me!"

Dove shakes her head. "No, I just thought you were William, that's all." She takes in Melissa's outfit. "You look amazing."

Melissa smooths out her dress. "Thanks."

Dove toys with the necklace, caught between wanting to stay in and a new feeling cropping up. Loneliness.

"Listen, it's my birthday . . . great necklace by the way."

"A gift from you know who," Dove says and then, catching up on Melissa's words, blurts, "You didn't mention this little fact? That as of today you are one whole year older? How could you have kept it a—"

Melissa interrupts. "I don't know. Maybe I just didn't want to deal with being twelve months older.

Or maybe I didn't want to celebrate that a year's gone by and I'm no closer to . . ."

"To what?"

"To—something. Look, I'm not going to bore you with my crap tonight. But come out with me." Melissa shoves a pair of navy blue pants toward Dove. She looks at them, considering whether she should wear them.

"So you do have some sort of party planned?"

Melissa shakes her head and then nods. "I don't, but Harley's throwing something small together. Come out with us."

"Us, you and Harley?"

Melissa pauses, biting on her lower lip. She'd told Max to wait in the car, knowing if they showed up together Dove would immediately say no. "Well, yes, me and Harley and . . . others." She looks away.

Dove ducks to meet Melissa's gaze. "Wait. Hold on. If Harley's in charge of the party, is she here with you?" Melissa shakes her head. "So who is the *we* with you?"

Melissa's mouth forms a perfect O. "Before you get angry, just listen . . ."

"You're with Max? He's here?" Dove tries to remain unaffected by this guess. She puts her hands on her hips. "No way am I willingly going out with him." *Gone are the days of being casual friends with him, way gone are the days of flirting with him, and a bit too close are the days of nearly ruining everything with William for him.*

Melissa looks pissed off. "It's my birthday and he's been nice enough to let me stay with him and he's driving to the party. What's the crime in that?"

Dove shouts, "You're staying with him? What next, you're going to announce your engagement?" A flush overtakes her pale cheeks. *Where is this coming from?* Dove wonders. *Why get so upset over nothing? Unless it's something.*

Melissa crosses her arms over her chest. "It's not like that."

"Well, how is it, then?"

Melissa starts to crack up, the laughter welling up inside her until it spills out of her mouth, causing her eyes to water. "You . . ."

"What?"

"Don't you even see it?" She makes Dove pivot so she can see her reflection in the tiny square mirror, its edges crackled with rust.

"See what?"

"Every time Max's name gets mentioned you freak out."

"So?" Dove notes the rise in color in her face, the way her heart slams into her chest.

"So . . . it's just something I've noticed. You have

an inability to be rational around him. Around his name and around his being." Melissa looks amused.

"Oh, shut up," Dove says jokingly. She takes a breath, reeling in any stray emotions. "I want to celebrate your birthday, but not with him. Sometimes a response is all it is, nothing more."

"Fine. Don't come out with us, but don't be pissed about me staying at the Sugar Hut, either. It beats the hell out of this place." Melissa gestures to the rest of the crew quarters, the small berths, the splintering floor, the dank smell.

Dove thinks about William going out. About Melissa going out. About Harley being out and about Max heading out into the island night. And then about staying in. "It's not a choice," she says. "I have to stay in."

"To avoid dealing with Max?" Melissa raises her eyebrows suggestively.

"To get some sleep for tomorrow," Dove says. "But you have fun. Have a happy birthday! And fill me in on anything that I miss!"

16

As they drive to the birthday bash, Melissa tries to comfort Max, whose face is a vision of disappointment.

"She's not coming, but don't worry."

Max grips the steering wheel with both hands. "Don't tell me not to worry unless you think I still have a shot in hell with Dove."

"I think you do. Have a shot in hell, I mean. Not a big shot, but a small one."

Max manages a wry grin. "A tiny ray of hope?"

"Something like that," Melissa says. "And by the way, thanks for driving. And for letting me crash at your place . . . and for being . . ."

"A friend?" Max nudges her.

"Yeah." Instinctively she puts her fingers to her nose, checking to see if they still smell of onions from her hours of chopping and slicing before. She turns to Max. "Is it a huge turnoff if a girl smells like food?"

"Depends on the kind, doesn't it?" Max says, eyeing the road ahead. In the darkening air, the palm trees rustle and sway as the car veers left and then turns onto a gritty road.

"The kind of food or the kind of girl?" Melissa queries, thinking about Orange Shorts and the potential for a birthday wish come true.

"Both," Max says and swerves toward the beach to park the car.

As the car settles to a stop, Melissa's mouth drops open. In front of them is a huge open-air rotunda, looking like a photograph she'd seen of a Victorian seaside pier. "It's so beautiful," she gushes.

"Yeah—it's historic and you can rent it . . ." Max explains as they walk to the structure.

Billowing out from the posts of the rotunda is what seems like thousands of Mylar balloons. Strung up all across the inside are minuscule white lights that give the large circular space an air of magic. Off to the side, a steel drum band plays, sending music washing over everything.

"Harley! You goddess!" Melissa runs over and hugs her.

Harley smiles. "So you don't hate it?" She laughs. "I was worried it was too much." Melissa shakes her head, her eyes wide. "But then I thought, heck—you deserve it. Everyone deserves to be happy, right?"

Melissa nods, hugs her again, and says, "You are a transformed woman, Harley." Who'd have thought she'd go from bitter and ultra-cool to generous and giddy?

Harley waves to Max, who busies himself by the bar, and turns back to Melissa. "Okay—so . . . there is one thing, though."

Melissa tilts her head. "Oh, no. Why do I feel like you're about to . . ." Melissa looks around at the people filtering in. Coming up the dock are a group of girls, all in dresses. She looks more closely. All in green dresses. Over by the steel band, a couple of guys are bouncing to the beat—one in a green shirt, the other in yellow.

"Hey!" shout another group of people from one of the doorways. They, too, are in green, yellow, and—at the back—two in red.

"Something's weird," Melissa says. "You're in red."

"I love red," Harley grins, touching her bright red bias-cut dress. "But yeah, you're catching on quicker than I thought."

"The theme is color? Green?" Harley shakes her head. "Okay . . . green and yellow?"

"What's green, red, and yellow?" Harley demands. "Come on."

Melissa shrugs. "I have no clue."

Harley grabs a microphone from behind the bar and switches it on as the crowd thickens. "Welcome, everyone! And thanks for coming! I'd like to introduce the guest of honor—Melissa Forsythe. Please feel free to wish her a happy birthday and remember—this is a stoplight party, so get to it!" She puts the microphone down as people cheer and mingle, heading to the bar for drinks and to dance by the band.

"Get it?" Harley asks, grabbing Melissa and spinning her around. "You've got your majority in green—they're single. Then your yellow folks, and they're the ones who are dating but not serious, so it's okay to approach, and then you've got the dreaded red. Red is no go."

"As in stop."

"As in, yeah." Harley points. "Like him. But that's why I did it—you know, took the legwork out of it for you."

Melissa sighs and laughs at the same time. "You

don't think I'm capable of discerning for myself if someone's available? Am I that desperate?"

"No, not like that. I just wanted to save you time." Harley motions for a few servers to make their way into the crowd, stopping first to give Melissa a taste of the treats.

She nibbles on a shish kebab skewer crammed with roasted peppers in yellow, green, and red, and spicy shrimp. "You really know how to throw a party. Thanks."

"No problem," Harley says, her eyes distracted. "But I think I have to go!"

"You're leaving?" Melissa grabs her arm.

"No—just vacating temporarily." She thumbs into the crowd. "Bug's here and he's wearing red—for me." She bites her lower lip and smiles, showing her bright white teeth. "Enjoy."

Melissa ogles the crowd of partygoers that she doesn't know, the red-shirt-wearing boys and yellow-skirted girls, the multitudes of people in green holding tropical drinks in plastic cups of the same colors. With her own dress rustling against her legs in the ocean breeze, she looks into the crowd, letting her eyes sweep the faces of dancers and minglers until she sees him. At the back of the room, his body blocked by a swarm of people heading for the tables of food, is Orange Shorts.

Only, presumably this time he won't be wearing orange. A stoplight party. *And I should be in green, no doubt*, Melissa thinks as she accepts a fizzy drink from a tray. *Even though I feel yellow.*

Intent on seeing what color he's wearing, she keeps an eye on the crowd where Orange Shorts was, hoping for a glimpse of green. *Pine, leaf, kelly, chartreuse, anything will do,* Melissa thinks. *Just be green*.

At that moment, the crowd parts and Orange Shorts emerges from it. Melissa can't turn away now that he's obviously caught her looking, so she gives him a smile. He smiles back at her and her heart slides down into her toes. *Red. He's wearing red. Couldn't it have at least been yellow?*

Max saves her from wilting completely. "So, that's the guy who's got you swooning?"

"I'm not swooning," Melissa informs him as they dance. She tries not to spill her drink while music echoes all around her and fellow partygoers bump into her.

"Don't rush over to him," Max informs her.

"Oh, this from the king of successful romance."

"Touché. No, just give him a few minutes to ogle you."

"Why bother? He's in red."

Max shrugs. "I'm in white. Maybe he missed the memo. Maybe he's a true nonconformist and is very single but wearing red to prove a point."

"And what point would that be?"

Max shakes his head. "I have no clue."

Melissa concedes. "Well, when you put it that way . . . maybe I will go over. In a minute." She pauses, noticing something else. "And that should give you an opportunity to make your way to the bar."

"I have a drink," Max says. "Don't need another."

Melissa insists. "Yes. You do." She shoves him away from the dancing and toward the long bar.

"No, I—" Max stops short of disagreeing further when he sees Dove leaning on the bar, standing on tiptoe so she can reach a plastic umbrella.

"I guess she decided to come after all," Melissa says.

Max nods, his voice temporarily suspended from action. "Guess so."

"Hey, you!" Orange Shorts gives Melissa a hug. "Rumor has it you're a year older."

"I can confirm that rumor," Melissa says, trying to play fun and casual while unable to take her eyes off his shirt. *Red. Red. Red.*

"You wanna dance?" He looks into her eyes, a small smile playing at his lips.

Do I want to dance? Forever. But if I do, then I'll be drawn in even more than I already am. She thinks back to the water at the hot springs, to being with him and wanting more. "I can't," she says, her protection instincts rising up. "Not right now."

Orange Shorts swallows, nods, and sticks his hands in his pockets. "Maybe later?"

"Maybe," Melissa says, looking over his shoulder to see who his counterpart is—the lucky person who gets to dance with him on a regular basis.

Tucked into a small inlet a ways off the pier, Harley leans in for one more kiss with Bug.

"Nice-color dress, by the way," he says into her ear, pulling her close.

"I thought you'd approve." Harley plucks at Bug's shirt. "Not that you're Mr. Crimson yourself."

Bug wears a bright yellow long-sleeved T-shirt. He pulls back to look at Harley sheepishly. "I know. I know. I wanted to wear red. Of course . . ." He kisses her again.

"But?"

"But I'm also not the King of Laundry, so . . ."

"So . . ." Harley laughs and watches Bug's face for signs of dishonesty. *Why would he lie, though? He's with me. I'm with him. No color can disprove that.*

"So yellow was the next best thing. You told me the theme, and I wanted to respect it."

"Well," Harley says, touching her necklace from him, "I respect that you respect me."

Bug wraps his arms around her and they hug in the cooling air. "I could stay like this all night."

Currents of pleasure float over Harley. She nods. "I could, too, but . . . I should get in and check on things. The cake's a giant stoplight. I'm not sure where to put it."

Bug nods. "But I'll meet you later?"

"Of course," Harley says. "I'll wait for you at the usual time." She wishes, for once, that he'd invite her to his place, so she could see where he works and sleeps. *But maybe it's better this way. Why mess with a good thing?* She looks at his face and grins. *And this is definitely a good thing.*

As Max approaches Dove inside, where the festivities are, Melissa heads outside the rotunda to the pier. The wind is heavy, gusting in and lifting the silvery balloons into the night, though they stay tied to the posts and railing. Melissa feels disappointment ripple through her. *Orange Shorts isn't orange, he's red. Dove has her choice of two guys, Harley's got Bug, and I'm . . . I'm the same as usual. Pining away and not getting what I want.* She brushes a tear away, hating the self-pity. *Is it so much to ask for one simple birthday wish?*

She continues to lean on the railing, looking at the water below. *My hands smell like onions and it doesn't even matter—no one's going to get close enough to get a whiff of them.*

"You okay?" Dove asks her.

"Yeah, I'm fine." Melissa spins to look at Dove, who is dressed in white and looks lovely with the lights glowing behind her.

"You don't sound fine."

Melissa tugs at her hair. "I am. I'm okay. It's just . . ." *I don't even want to admit it. Saying your disappointment out loud only makes it more real.* Melissa turns to look over her shoulder and does a quick scan of the rotunda. "I'm glad you ended up coming out."

"Way to switch subjects, but thanks. I took a cab. It just didn't feel right not being here with you."

"But I thought you had to be up really early to impress the owner?"

Dove nods. "But at least I can give you a birthday hug."

"Were you hoping to see William?" Melissa feels a little tug asking Dove, but she figures it can't hurt.

Dove looks out at the water, her skin clear and bathed in the moonlight. "Not really. He said he was going out—but probably to the Bait and Tackle—some crappy dive over on the other side of the island."

"Did you look for him?" Melissa turns again, this time spotting Orange Shorts dancing with a girl in a red strappy dress. *So there's his girlfriend, the reason for the red clothing.* Melissa bites her lip.

"Sort of," Dove says. "But I kind of got sideswiped."

"Meaning?" Far off, Melissa can see Harley walking up the beach, her telltale hair and colt-long legs giving her away. *Where has she been?* Melissa wonders. *No doubt getting a birthday kiss even though it's not her day.*

"Meaning—nothing, I guess. I saw Max—he's . . . he looks . . ."

Melissa raises her eyebrows at Dove. "See? You're losing your ability to speak—all rational thought going out of your—"

"No. Not true. So he looks great. So he's smart and—"

"What'd you guys talk about?" Melissa asks, wondering if Max put into action a grand plan of getting Dove to fall for him once and for all.

"Books." Dove looks serene as she goes on. "That book I was reading on the plane? He's read it. Studied it. We just talked about that."

"About love?" Melissa pokes Dove in the ribs.

"About the academic idea of love," Dove corrects.

"Well, it sounds like quite a class discussion." Melissa stands up and tucks her hair behind her ears, smoothing out her dress and getting ready to head into the rotunda and take advantage of not being the one who has to work tonight. *Why should I skip the food, wine, and cake just because I'm lovelorn? Having a bad case of unrequited crushing isn't the end of the world.* She takes a few steps away. "Do you ever regret not being with him—Max, I mean?"

Dove licks her lips and ruffles her hair. "Maybe?" She thinks about lying in the cramped bed with William. "No?" She thinks about William not meeting her at the airport, about his lack of interest in her academic dreams, his wanting to go out all the time instead of staying in with her. "Yes?" She shakes her head. Then she touches her necklace. "No. No, I don't. William's perfect for me."

Melissa nods. "Good. Because regret sucks." She

thinks about how much easier it would be if she hadn't bumped into Orange Shorts when she lost her flip-flop. How much simpler it would be if they hadn't had so much fun and connection at the hot springs. But at the end of the day, did it matter? *I owe him a dance. And I'll be damned if I'm letting one last shot at being near him pass me by.* "I'm heading inside to dance with someone before I have more regret."

"I'm going to flag a taxi. There's a whole line of them waiting at the top of the road. Happy, happy birthday! May you get your wish," Dove says as she walks off.

"We'll see," Melissa says and gives a flick of her eyebrows and a sly smile.

17

The night verges on becoming morning, and Melissa works her way over to the dessert table, where soon her birthday cake will be on display for everyone to see and eat.

"William!" she says, surprised at first to see him. "What are you doing here?"

"Isn't everyone on the island here?" His gold-tipped hair matches his shirt. "Happy, happy, by the way." He gives her a friendly pat on the back.

"You just missed Dove," Melissa says. *Probably a good thing, since you're not exactly sporting the red you should be.*

William's mouth opens as though he's surprised. "Really?" He looks around the room.

"She took a cab back to the boat."

William lets out a sigh. "Oh. Well . . . I'll see her at the Botanical Gardens thing, anyway."

"Emmy Taylor's?" Melissa questions. *Why would they wait until then to get together? Is Dove delusional? Or is their relationship just mellower than I thought?*

"Yeah. Sounds like a fun night."

Melissa suddenly thinks the fact that William isn't wearing red is a big warning flag of the same color. "Um, William?"

"Yeah?" He bounces to the music. "You know what's so great about Dove?" he adds. "She's a free spirit."

Melissa considers this. "Really? I don't see her like that. . . . Granted, I haven't known her as long as you have. But she seems more . . . more like she wishes she were a free spirit." Then she worries that this came out wrong. "I mean, I have a friend who is definitely a free spirit," Melissa says, thinking of Harley. "And she can fly off anywhere or do anything and not worry about it. And I think even though Dove likes adventure, she does worry."

William nods, his voice a bit unsteady. "Maybe so. Maybe I'm confusing her with . . ." He stops. "It's just—she and I had a lot of time apart, you know? Phone calls and e-mails."

Melissa understands. "So being together in person is better than e-mail?" She feels silly but isn't up to having such a big conversation with William when all she wants to do is find Orange Shorts and dance with him. "Of course it is."

"How many times have I written LilydeDove at blah blah blah? Too many times."

"LilydeDove?"

"Yeah, the other name she wanted was taken. Glad I got my address so long ago."

"Why, what is it? SurferBoy at something something? Or, no, Boating Babe?" Melissa jokes.

William looks around at the stoplight colors as Harley emerges from the back room rolling a metal cart on top of which sits a three-tiered cake—one layer yellow, one green, one red. The candles are not lighted yet. "Nah, my e-mail's much simpler and less revealing."

"What is it?" Melissa asks. A few feet away, Orange Shorts appears, this time with the red-dressed girl he was dancing with off to his side rather than in his arms. Melissa's gut clenches.

"Mine's thebug@islandmail.com."

"Oh," Melissa says, her eyes and heart pulled away from the talk with William. Then something creeps into her mind, recalling the mix-up she'd had with names back at Les Trois. "How'd you get that address?" Melissa asks but as the words come out, she has a sinking feeling.

"It's my nickname from childhood. No one knows to call me it now, but as a kid people called me Bug." William's words confirm Melissa's worst suspicions.

She opens her mouth to protest. "You're . . ."

"I'm Bug," William says, shaking her hand. "But forget you heard it. It's a secret name."

You bet it is, Melissa thinks, her mind racing, her insides fuming as she tries to figure out the best way to proceed. *Harley's with Bug. Dove's with William. William is Bug. I'm going to just tell him off right now.* She grabs him before he walks away, but then pauses, wanting certain clarification before she accuses him.

"Wait . . . just so I have it on record—"

"Record?" William looks at her like she's nuts.

"Whatever. The point is—does anyone call you Bug now?" *Please say no, please say no.*

"No," he confirms. "No one would ever call me that now." William looks down at his hands, then shoves them in his pockets.

Melissa sighs deeply. *Oh thank God. He's not a lame cheating ass. He's just William.* "Looks like it's nearly cake time for me," she says. *See? All a big misunder-*

standing. That's why you always need to probe further and ask. She smiles.

"No one would call me Bug," William reiterates, grinning, ". . . unless I met someone incredibly special. Then she'd be the one person to call me Bug."

The smile on Melissa's face fades. She feels her stomach turn, knowing that despite her rambunctious nature, there's no way Harley is in on the duplicity. *If only Dove hadn't been so damn secretive with her precious photos of William back at Les Trois, maybe none of this would have happened. But Dove had stashed her pictures away. And Harley keeps lots of details to herself.*

She stands with her hands at her sides, wishing she didn't know all this, wishing she didn't have to meet up quite so soon with both Harley and Dove, who clearly were—despite the hundreds of white lights around them—in the dark about this.

"So, how about that dance?" Orange Shorts lets his palm linger on Melissa's bare shoulder.

Melissa wishes she didn't feel every pore of his skin on hers, each molecule drawing her further into the air around him. "Um, sure." The haze of information from William engulfs her and the distraction makes her face bland.

"If you don't want to . . ."

Melissa jolts back to reality. "No—it's not that. I do want to dance . . . I just . . . why are guys such lying creeps sometimes?" Melissa allows herself to be led to the dance floor.

"I can't speak for all of my gender, but I'll venture to say—because we don't know any better?"

Melissa puts her hands around his neck, for a second leaning into the dance and then remembering the red dress, his red shirt. She speaks up, her voice brash and laced with sarcasm. "Take you, for example. You come off all interesting with your hot springs scenarios and your banter and your . . . your . . ." She falters, looking into his eyes. "But then you're here and wearing red and with the girl in the dress . . ." Melissa lets her hands drop, standing amid the dancing couples and feeling foolish.

He stares at her for a minute and then taps her shoulder as if cutting in on her misery. "Pardon me. Melissa?"

"Yeah?"

He waves the girl in the red dress over. She appears in front of them, looking tall, with honey-streaked hair and bronzed skin, and smiles. "This is my sister."

Melissa suddenly feels herself turn the color of a sign—a red sign. The blush takes over her face. "So why the red shirt?"

"Nice to meet you, Melissa. Happy birthday. I'm Bethany."

"Hi, Bethany." Melissa's voice is octaves lower than normal. *The sister? Okay, feeling a little lame now . . .*

Bethany takes a look at Melissa and back at her brother. "I'm guessing this is the girl?" He nods.

I'm the girl? What girl? The girl he is madly in love with? The girl who reeks of onions? The girl he spent so much time with and yet whose name he never divulged?

"Yeah," he says. "This is the girl that I was telling you about. The one who ran away from me on the beach today . . ."

Bethany nods and leaves the two of them to talk. "So you saw me today?" Melissa asks.

"Of course I did. You saw me, too."

Melissa's chest feels as though it could cave in on itself, her legs wobbling. "So why the red then? I saw and I thought—"

"Because I met you. So what's the point in wearing green if the one I want to be with is right here?"

"That's probably one of the most romantic things anyone's ever said to me." Melissa can't tear her eyes away from his mouth.

"Not *the* most romantic?" He grins.

She thinks back to Gabe on the mountain. *What had he said? Something romantic. Very romantic.* She pushes him out of her mind, concentrating on the steel drum version of "The Way You Look Tonight."

He reaches out for her and she's about to go to him when an abrupt grab pulls her away.

"What the—" Melissa looks up to find Max, breathing hard as if he has something important to say. She looks at Orange Shorts. "Sorry. This is my friend, Max. He's— Can you just hold the dance idea for one sec?" She clutches his arm and feels flustered. "I'll be right back."

As she stands talking to Max on the side of the room, Melissa looks back fervently to where her dance was cut short. "This isn't really the best time, Max."

"Well, sorry," Max says. "But I needed to talk."

"More?" Melissa asks, her memory fresh from the marathon talkage that Max had spewed the night she first slept at the Sugar Hut.

"I wanted to say . . . it's your birthday. And you—you're a nice person."

Melissa stares at him blankly. "Thanks."

"And I just wanted to tell you that, in case I don't see you."

"What?" Melissa stops, looks at the dance floor and the impending cake table, and looks at Max. "What do you mean?"

"I'm done with it." He gestures with his arms around the room. "I mean," he says, slugging his drink, "that I'm leaving. Cutting ties. Heading back to Oxford early to find solace in my books. Got the chance to talk with Dove about books tonight, as a matter of fact . . ."

"I know, and she said—"

Max interrupts. "Didn't Shakespeare say . . . oh, never mind. The point is, I'm through trying to reach her." He looks at the couples dancing, their arms moving to the music's beat. Melissa follows his gaze and sees Bug—otherwise known as William—talking to Harley by the cake.

Seeing him with her makes Melissa's mouth twist into a frown. But it's not Harley's fault. It's not Dove's. It's his—and only his. *Still, why do I have to be the one to know all this? Maybe sometimes people don't divulge things not because they're lying, like William Bug, but because they're scared. I should have spoken up at the hot springs and I didn't.* "Don't."

Max furrows his brow. "Huh?"

"Don't go. Or, if you have to go, go." Melissa flings her hand toward the ground. "But at least tell her first."

"Tell her what, exactly?"

"Anything. Everything. Just spill it."

"I've done that before, if you recall . . . and it didn't—"

Melissa eyes the crowd, looking for Orange Shorts. When she doesn't see him, she feels slightly frantic. "Just do it once more, okay? Remember what I said about grand gestures? Give the girl a little drama." As opposed to a necklace, Melissa thinks, making a face when she sees Harley playing with the silver necklace clasped around her neck and realizes that it's the same one Dove had on this evening.

"Now?" Max looks prepared to bolt.

Melissa thinks. "No. Not now. At Emmy Taylor's party this weekend."

"Ah, the infamous Botanical Gardens extravaganza." Max looks doubtful. "And why, pray tell, should that be the chosen locale for my last effort in soul-baring?"

"Because," Melissa says, patting Max on the back, "if you gotta get the girl—or try to—you might as well have a gorgeous backdrop."

Max nods. "That, my friend, is true."

Melissa knows she's not a free spirit and as a result, she does worry that the moment she was in the middle of having with her true crush is over. *And I don't even know his name to yell it, even if I wanted to make a grand gesture myself right now.*

"Melissa?"

She swivels to face him. "Yes, Orange Shorts? You see, if I'm honest, which I'm going to be now that I know why you're wearing red . . . I don't know your name."

"So?"

"So, it's weird." Melissa looks into his green eyes. "I don't know your name but I feel like I know you."

"Exactly my point," he says and resumes the dance. "Looks like you're about to blow out the candles."

Melissa feels a giant smile brighten her face. Nothing could make this moment better. "So, will you tell me it or not?"

"My name?" He leans in to brush the hair back from her face, sending rows of shivers down her arms. "When the time is right, of course."

Melissa feels elated, not by the fact that she still doesn't know what to call him, but because despite the way things started, the night is turning out okay. "Want to be my date to the Botanical Gardens?"

He nods. "I'll wear red, blue, or whatever color you want me to."

He pulls her to the dance floor for a twirl. They laugh and trade remarks, easing right back into their banter from the hot springs.

"So, admit it, you've missed me every second you're not with me," he says.

Not missing a beat, Melissa answers, "I hardly noticed when you were around."

"Oh, come on. You've loved me from the minute you saw me at the hot springs . . ."

"Oh, I love you now?" Melissa jokes. "Fine. You're onto me—you're right. Except it wasn't at the springs."

"Oh no?"

Melissa shakes her head, her true emotions rising to the surface so that she can't keep up the act anymore. "I should get cake—Harley wants me to cut the cake."

"Wait—wait a second . . . when did you see me first?"

Melissa shrugs. *What is the point of keeping everything bottled up?* "FINE—I saw you at the dock. You don't remember but . . ."

"Of course I do," Orange Shorts says, his grip on her waist tightening. "You lost a flip-flop and I gallantly offered to get it . . . but you beat me to it. Only that wasn't the first time."

Melissa thinks back. "No, I'm sure it was."

Orange Shorts turns her chin so her eyes are locked on his. "I was there, at the airport . . ." Melissa looks dubious. "You lost your luggage. You had on . . . those same flips-flops . . ."

"I've been wearing them nonstop."

"But you did lose your luggage, right? You stood there staring at a poster of Matty Chase. . . ." He looks at her for a reaction.

"I adore Matty Chase. And I work for him now. How's that for serendipity?" Melissa plays with a ringlet of her hair.

"That *is* some big serendipity." He nods, looking temporarily derailed, his face flushed. "I was at the airport to pick up Bethany—she'd missed her flight the day before. I watched you waiting as all the bags went around . . ."

"And?" Melissa feels her blood racing around her body, fights the urge to grab him.

"And I kept thinking, how come she's waiting for bags—these inanimate objects—and I'm waiting for . . ." He takes her hands, kisses them, pauses and looks at her, no doubt smelling the onion.

"For?"

"For her. For you." He pulls her in as the music dwindles and kisses her. A rousing "Happy Birthday" starts up, and the song, the sound of waves crashing outside the rotunda, the stop, slow, and go colors swirling around her—it's all enough. Enough to make Melissa forget that she's the sole bearer of infidelity news for Dove and for Harley. It's enough to make her forget her onion-infused hands. Enough to make her let go of any question she has about where she's going in the future and instead be happy that one of her wishes, for right now, has come true.

18

Having slaved all night after returning from the birthday bash, Dove is exhausted. Her small hands ache, and her eyes are weary, and yet her pulse still races. *Everything has to be perfect—just right so there's no way I can get sacked and sent packing.* In the morning light, she studies the array of food she's worked on: miniature fruit tarts, each one glazed with melted sugar and topped with local berries, mint framboise gelée in champagne flutes, looking elegant and fresh, a large bowl of vanilla baked bread pudding with a chocolate sauce for the side, and freshly braided bread served with cheeses she managed to buy from a local goat farmer at cost. *I'll impress everyone not only with the cooking but with my frugality.* She gives a self-satisfied smile as she displays all the food on the long buffet table inside.

"I don't want to miss any of the sunny morning," the owner, Davina Wallop, says in passing as she snatches a mug of coffee from the table and heads outside. Without further elaborating, she manages to convey that breakfast should be served outside. In her navy blue swimsuit and stark white cover-up paired with simple flats that look as though they've come from a street cart but, Dove knows, have been custom-made, Davina looks every inch the boatside diva.

Dove stands near all of the fresh foods, taking a breath before she tackles the job of moving everything yet again to the outside eating area. *Of course, there are no fresh flowers out there like there are inside, and no tablecloths, but fine. I'll do my best.*

As Davina reads her copy of the *Financial Times* and waves to a few friends trotting down the dock, she glances at Dove from the corner of her eye. "Why didn't you set up here in the first place?"

Dove uses her formal voice as she steadies the platter of fruit on the still dew-damp white table. "The forecast called for rain. I didn't want to have the breakfast ruined by—"

"Rain can hardly *ruin* anything—it's not as though

I melt . . ." Davina says, but before she can continue she goes to greet her friends.

With an image of the Wicked Witch of the West melting after water is poured on her, Dove tries to get past the initial disruption and focus on the tasks at hand. *It's one meal. It's one job—just prove to her I'm worth having in the galley, and that's all. Then I'll be free to get back to my life—cooking, reading, and trying to figure out just what to do about William.* Before she can get distracted by thoughts of him, by thoughts of what their date at the Botanical Gardens will be like, Dove hears her name in passing.

As she rearranges the bread pudding, making sure the chafing dish it's in stays warm, Dove overhears Davina apologize for the food not already being out, and the guests nod while looking at Dove as though she's incompetent. Dove lets the criticism slide off her, knowing she will woo them with her wares.

Gus appears, helping Dove by wiping off the extra tables and chairs and setting them up in a social circle, then offering each guest coffee or tea. But rather than accept further help, Dove shakes her head—she doesn't want Davina and her friends to get the wrong impression.

"I don't need your help. But thanks, Gus," Dove says quietly to him when he drags a chair across the deck.

Gus looks at her for a second and then shrugs. "Suit yourself."

Dove smiles at the guests and brings the last of the food from the inside dining room to the deck, where the guests have seated themselves around the table.

Dove and Davina lock eyes. Davina raises her eyebrows. "Well?"

Dove stands with her hands clasped behind her back, her clean apron tied in a bow, her hair held back from her face with a wide light blue band. "I'm pleased to announce that breakfast is served." She gestures to the sideboard, where all of the trays and dishes are artfully arranged.

The guests wait for Davina to speak. "Well, then serve us."

Dove feels anxiety rise within her chest. Without disrespecting her boss, she tries to show the array of food. "It's a big buffet. That way everyone can choose what they like."

Davina makes a noise that sounds somewhere between a cough and a sigh. "We'd like to be served. This isn't a roadside pancake house." She rolls her eyes at her friends.

Dove swallows a breath of air and her pride and begins, wordlessly, to bring around each of the dishes, scooping modest amounts of each type of food onto the plates.

"Don't be stingy," Davina scolds while smiling—seemingly immune to the fact that she's insulting Dove. "Heap it on. That is, unless you haven't made enough."

"There should be plenty," Dove says. The sun's rays beat down on her as she brings tray after bowl to the table. She can feel perspiration welling up in her bra and her face flushes with effort and worry. *This is not what I planned. This isn't even close to how I pictured the meal going.* She takes a minute to collect herself by the tall glasses of mint iced tea. *In fact, none of this is what I pictured. What was it, exactly, that I wanted? To shack up with William in a beach hut?* Dove grimaces as she realizes that her island fantasies were slightly unrealistic, just one long string of images of her and William in the sand as the sun set, their hands intertwined.

"Excuse me, Dove? When you've got a minute?" Davina snaps, as though Dove's a dog, and waits for a response.

"Yes, of course." Dove comes over and leans down to hear what Davina has to say.

"The bread pudding is delicious," Davina says. Her friends agree, nodding and giving words of encouragement about the whole meal. Dove's spirits immediately rise, her smile engaging her features, instantly relieved.

Relieved, that is, until Davina suddenly stands up, gasping and clutching her stomach.

"Oh, I . . . uhh . . . oh God . . ." Davina's face contorts in pain.

Dove rushes to her. 'What? What is it?"

Davina, still doubled over, her face bright red, glares at Dove. "The ingredients . . ."

Confused for a minute, Dove then clues in. "In the bread pudding? It's pretty standard." Her heart beats too fast, her legs feel wobbly. What's going on? "Are you okay?"

One of Davina's friends stands up to help. "Just tell her the ingredients, Cook."

"My name's Dove." Realizing that no one cares, Dove thinks back. "Baguette slices, milk, chocolate, vanilla extract—it's all pretty standard."

"Vanilla . . ." Davina seethes.

"Vanilla extract," Dove says slowly, wondering what she's done wrong. Trying to cover any mistake, she adds, "And it's the good stuff, Tahitian vanilla. I find it's richer, more—"

Davina stands up, clutching the railing for support, her face now more green than red. "I cannot have Tahitian vanilla. It's processed with a certain kind of . . ." She pauses, bringing her hand to her mouth. "It makes me . . ."

Sick. Dove suddenly recalls the first day, arriving

and all the information Gus spewed at her. Under specifications about food likes and dislikes, Dove thought she'd committed to memory all of Davina's tastes—no boysenberry, eggs served soft- not hard-boiled, no use of macadamia nuts. Then she sees Davina actually spewing her breakfast over the side of the boat as her friends begin to disperse.

A sinking feeling overwhelms Dove's body. *Was there a note about Tahitian vanilla and its effect on Davina's stomach?* Then Dove gets a visual image—a highlighted sentence—*Tahitian vanilla causes instant vomiting. How could I have missed that? Who forgets instant vomiting?* Despite the heat of the day creeping in, Dove gets a chill. *This is bad. Worse than bad. Terrible.*

Gus appears and leads Davina toward the master cabin, shooting Dove a look that tells her this was no ordinary mistake.

"That's the last of them," Harley says when she's folded the newly arrived white T-shirts and displayed them on the table next to a stack of coiled belts and a bowl full of faux-jewel rings. *Of course,* she thinks, *these ones look faux, but are real.* She picks up an oval-shaped ruby ring, slides it on her middle finger, and studies the way it looks against her tanned skin.

"Nice job with the shirts, Harlan," says her co-worker Annie, who insists on using her full name. "But put the ring back."

Harley shrugs. "Why? It looks good. Besides, you've got a scarf on that I know full well you haven't bought."

Annie blushes and touches the fringed silk. "I actually just did—you can check the records if you want." She coughs suggestively.

"What's that supposed to mean?" Harley asks, defensive already. She goes to the cash register where they keep the books. A separate book for staff purchases is off to the side.

Annie looks at Jen, another associate, who wears a matching outfit to Annie's. "Nothing—it's just . . ."

"What? Just spit it out. It's not like I won't have heard it before." Angrily, Harley begins sorting through a new shipment of shoes, ordering the boxes by size so she can move them to the back room.

"Well," Annie says, "we've just been noticing . . ."

"We?" Harley asks. Her throat goes dry but she keeps sorting the shoes.

"The staff—some of us."

"And Mrs. Taylor?" Harley asks, drumming up the name of the owner who came in daily under the pretense of checking on everything but really wanted to snag new outfits for the party circuit before taking up her preferred spot at the café down the street.

Annie busies herself with the books. "Um, yes. Mrs. Taylor did notice. I mean, the woman has eyes and ears all over the world, right?"

"Meaning?" Harley grimaces.

"Meaning—she owns stores all over the place and has spies—I don't know? Anyway, she was at some party last night? And saw you?" Annie's sentences all go up at the end, making her sound continually flustered, which annoys Harley.

Harley stops sorting shoes, pausing to think back. "Which party?"

"Some party at the rotunda near here? A birthday?"

Harley's throat enters desert status, so dry she can barely swallow. She'd taken the dress from Pulse after everyone had gone, balled it up in her bag and smoothed it on only once she'd reached the party. No one was invited from here. No one would notice. Or, correction: No one was meant to. "So?" is the best Harley can muster.

"So," Annie says, sighing, "even though you're the best folder, and probably the most convincing salesperson? She's pissed."

Harley bites her top lip. "And just what am I accused of?" She knows better than to admit fault before she has to.

Jen, less unsure of herself than Annie, steps forward. "Let's just say that when I went back and looked at the books—which she made me do—I noticed that you haven't actually bought anything with your staff discount."

"So that's a crime?" Harley puts her hands on her hips. "Did it ever occur to you that maybe I don't want to waste my meager earnings on this overpriced crap?" She grabs a shoe and flings it across the store. It lands with a thud by the front door, where a very angry and stern-looking Mrs. Taylor stands looking decidedly unflustered.

She bends down and picks up the shoe. "Annie, please put this in the proper box." Annie does as she's told while Harley stands there embarrassed, wishing she'd had more control over her mouth.

"My main concern, Harlan," Mrs. Taylor says as she surveys the store, "isn't the dress you—ahem—appear to have borrowed last night."

Harley wonders how on earth Mrs. Taylor would know. *Maybe the woman does have spies.* She wasn't at Melissa's birthday party, and no one from the store came, so who would report back? Mrs. Taylor walks past the racks of gauzy dresses and neatly organized swimsuits and hands a piece of paper to Harley. "This is for you."

Harley wonders what it could be. A notice she's

fired? An invitation? A ticket to somewhere else? She takes the bright red slip of paper and reads the words on it. *Citation for improper use of a public space*. "A fine of fifteen hundred dollars?" Harley can't believe it. Her tone is one of shock and dismay. *And hand-delivered, too,* Harley thinks as she grips the paper. Clearly, Mrs. Taylor was well connected.

"Apparently, one must go through the proper channels to rent the rotunda." Mrs. Taylor looks smug as she relays this. "This is a small island, Harlan, but we do things in accordance with tradition here. You can't just sidestep a rule . . ."

"I threw a friend a birthday party. I didn't think—"

"No. You didn't." Mrs. Taylor, now over by the cash register, flips open one of the oversized ledger books, scanning the lines until she points to one. "Just as you didn't think when you charged thousands of dollars' worth of clothing and accessories to a certain Mrs. de Rothschild."

Harley's breath comes out in jagged waves. De Rothschild. Dove's parents. "I know them," Harley says, stretching the truth. "They told—"

"They did no such thing."

Harley does a quick inventory of the problem. *How does she know? Who is Mrs. Taylor to say what Dove's parents would allow?* Sure that this is one of those situations where she's being bullied, Harley goes on. "The de Rothschilds are old friends of my family . . ." Harley winces inside, knowing that her trailer park upbringing would never amount to an old friendship with one of England's finest families. *But Dove's a close friend, right? Doesn't that count? She'll help me get out of this.*

"Well, then you'll have every opportunity to greet them shortly."

Harley's hands begin to shake. "Who?"

Mrs. Taylor pats the ledger book. "The de Rothschilds. They've come back to the island." She raises her eyebrows and watches Harley's face for a reaction. "I invited them to the Botanical Gardens party my daughter's throwing."

"Your daughter?" Harley feels foolish, just now putting the pieces together. Emmy Taylor, the glamorous girl who'd invited half the island to the upcoming festivities. Of course she's Mrs. Taylor's daughter. And of course Emmy had been at Melissa's bash last night, seen the dress, and reported back. Harley tries her best to fix things. "I can explain. I had to borrow the dress—I didn't . . . I don't . . ."

"You borrowed it?" Mrs. Taylor crosses her arms over her chest, waiting for a better explanation. "So presumably it's back where it should be?"

Harley falters, remembering that the dress is not,

in fact, on the rack, but rather in a heap on the floor of her cramped room, coated in sand from when she and Bug had watched the sunrise together on the beach. "I need to clean it first."

Mrs. Taylor sighs and walks calmly over so she's face-to-face with Harley while Annie and Jen try not to watch, moving the shoeboxes to the storage room. "I had every confidence in you when you started." She touches Harley's shoulder. "You look the part, certainly."

Harley smiles, hoping this is a rough patch like there always are in jobs, and that it will pass. "I value my job here, and I—"

"As I was saying," Mrs. Taylor interrupts, making it clear that she's in charge. "I have a sense of people. I pride myself on it, actually. And I had a good feeling about you. Your sales track is stronger in the short time you've been here than the other staff . . ."

Harley drinks in the praise, knowing that retail does suit her, that she's destined for some sort of career like this. "I was a chalet host—and then a waitress—and this job combines both. It's like I'm guiding people to the clothing they're meant to own."

Mrs. Taylor nods, then gives Harley a saddened look. "A perfect response." Harley grins. "Which is why it pains me to fire you. But as you know, if I let people, even people who work here, borrow clothing,

I wouldn't make any money." Mrs. Taylor smooths her blunt-cut dark hair and plucks a yellow opal ring from the bowl. "Integrity, above all else, is what matters in life. At a job, in a friendship, everything." She hands Harley the yellow ring. "Consider this a parting gift."

Harley holds the ring in her hand. Mrs. Taylor starts out of the store and Harley wonders if maybe this nightmare isn't really happening. No job yet again, an extra fifteen hundred dollars' worth of debt, and no idea what to do next. Mrs. Taylor stops at the door but instead of going out of it herself, she holds it open for Harley. "Ready?"

Harley walks to the door, pauses long enough to hand the ring back to Mrs. Taylor, and heads out. *Am I ready? No. But do I have integrity? Yes.* Harley walks up the cobblestone path, unsure where she'll wind up but knowing she'll have to deal with her monetary fine, her joblessness, and telling Dove that her parents are in town. *If I'm going to be honest and full of integrity, I might as well start with Dove*, she thinks. *I should go find her right now and warn her about the upcoming parental storm. After all, if my nutty mother were coming to find me, I'd want as much advance warning as possible.* Harley's feet shuffle on the cobblestones, her arms warm in the sun. She pictures Dove's easy manner, her soft and gentle ways, and wonders how she'll cope with her past creeping up on her. *She'll be fine*, Harley assures herself. *Isn't that what Dove's always saying—that she can handle anything?* And instead of heading toward the docks to find her friend, Harley looks one more time over her shoulder at Pulse and starts off to find the one person who can comfort her. Bug.

19

With the rippling rays of sunshine spreading across the infinity pool at the Sugar Hut, Melissa can almost forget about the nagging guilt. *It's not like I'm the one to blame,* she thinks, dwelling on Dove's and Harley's overlapping love interest while reaching for the sunblock.

"Here, let me." Orange Shorts grins as he squirts a dollop of lotion onto his palm and begins rubbing it into Melissa's neck. "Think you'll ever get your luggage back?" he asks, plucking at Melissa's makeshift bathing suit—a pair of surfer shorts rolled up at the waist and a threadbare white tank top layered over a blue one.

"Think you'll ever tell me your name?" Melissa volleys, tipping back so she can see her ultimate island fantasy, albeit upside down. It's taken every bit of resolve she has to be relaxed enough not to bombard him with questions about who he is, where he's from, and all the usual info people exchange. "Just one thing—that's all I ask. A name."

He finishes with the sunblock, applying the remnants to his own face, and leans back on the lounge chair. He and Melissa are the only ones by the pool, despite the glorious day. Max and his family have gone off to visit some friends at their private estate, leaving Melissa to enjoy the riches that the house has to offer: stocked fridge, clean pool, perfect day. "I'm not trying to be mysterious," he says. "I just think that people put too much emphasis on the exterior of things and lose sight of what's important. For example—I don't know your name."

"Not true."

"Fine. Melissa Forsythe. So I do know it." He smiles. "But I don't know your middle name."

"No way." Melissa shakes him off. "Not telling."

"Fine." He turns away, grinning but determined not to break his position.

"But names are important," Melissa says, swinging her feet over the edge of her chair so she can face him. She looks at his glistening arms, his chest rising and falling with each easy breath. "You've got to be something like Devonshire or Fulton or Weston. Some eclectic thing."

"Weston?" He raises his eyebrows and flicks some of the condensation from his glass of iced tea at her.

Melissa shrugs. "If you'd tell me your real name I wouldn't have to guess."

He sits up and turns so their knees touch. Melissa's hands shake just slightly with the warmth coming from his body to hers. It's all enough to make her mind leave behind the worries about being the bearer of bad news to Dove and Harley. *They'll rip each other to shreds*, Melissa thinks, the worry slipping back in. *And all over some guy who two-timed them both.* "Names do matter. A lot." Melissa looks at the pool, rising up so she can feel its water on her legs, take a dunk before she has to make her way to the restaurant for a long shift. "I have a friend . . . or, I mean, I know someone who lied about his name and—well, let's just say it got him into some trouble."

"Oh yeah?" Orange Shorts joins Melissa poolside, his perma-grin turned into a frown. "And that's what you're worried about?"

Melissa shakes her head. "I'm worried about other things, but maybe that, too. I mean, how do I know you without knowing you?"

"Nice sentence." He sits next to her on the cool flagstone, swishing his feet in the clear water. "Okay. Fine. In the interest of not being taken as a deceitful person." He dips his hand into the water and then rests his wet palm on Melissa's thigh. She doesn't flinch or move, just enjoys the feel of it on her skin. She waits, looking into his eyes, for him to reveal the big mystery. "Bob."

"Bob?" The laughter begins slowly, then rises up, erupting from her mouth. "Bob? As in just *b-o-b*? All this time I've been inventing exciting names and the personas to go along with them and here you are—"

"Just plain Bob. Yeah. Well, I never promised you anything odd or different." He moves his hand from her leg to her face. "Come—let's jump in before I drive you to the watering hole."

Melissa is about to jump in when she suddenly pauses. Bob waits for her in the water, holding his hands out so she'll meet him. "How'd you know about the fishing hole?" She squints at Bob and thinks back to a conversation she had with the wait-staff during one of her first shifts. They'd gone over the various restaurant slang—*eighty-sixing* something meant there was no more of it, as in eighty-six the grilled snapper, *the vault* was the big walk-in fridge, and *TACs* were totally annoying customers who sent things back. *The watering hole* was waiter-speak for the tiny break room at the far back of the kitchen, set apart from the rest of the place by the fact that it literally floated on a separate dock. It was where waiters and cooks kept books or magazines, snacks, and lots of iced coffee for refueling between shifts or taking orders. "What are you, like a connoisseur of all terms restaurant-o-lific?"

Bob gives a small laugh from the side of his mouth, reaching again for Melissa. She swears she can see him blush. "Let's just say I've put in some time of my own at various dining establishments. And rumor has it you're quite the kitchen catch." He flicks water at her from his hand.

"Oh, really? Could have fooled me." Melissa thinks about Olivia and how the staff seem to dislike her. But maybe that's changing.

"Nah, I'm sure you're great at what you do in the back of the house."

"*Back of the house* meaning kitchen. More slang." Melissa squints, wanting to pester him for more information, to dig up any remaining mystery about his past, about her presence in the rumor mill. But then she says his name—Bob—in her head. Such a simple, everyday name. *And does knowing it change anything?* She shakes her head. *I don't need to know more. I just need to be with him and enjoy myself.*

"Fine." Melissa smiles. "First this watering hole and then the other." She and Bob clasp hands and he pulls her gently into the sun-warmed water where they can talk and swim the next hour away before work beckons.

20

"Can I help you?" asks the salesgirl at Pulse as Dove scans the racks.

Brightly hued scarves, knee-length shorts, and poppy-colored dresses artfully arranged look beautiful, but none of them are what Dove's looking for. "No, thanks. Just browsing." Dove touches a flimsy shirt, checking the price tag and then letting it go. *I never used to do that. Checking the tag was for people with nothing in their wallets.* Well aware of her own emptying pockets, Dove wanders the store, not sure why she's here. *Maybe because I have nothing else to do. Maybe because I'm fired after the Tahitian vanilla disaster. Maybe because all I really want to do is curl up with my textbook and write down my thoughts. But what good would that do?* she wonders, nearly aloud. *It's not as though I have a place to hand in a paper, even if I did write it.*

"We have a new shipment of headbands," the salesperson offers. "They'd look great with your cropped hair." She fetches a pale blue flowered headband with a wide strap and hands it to Dove.

Out of courtesy, Dove slips it on, pushing it far back off her forehead. She glances in the mirror, trying to shrug off the errors of the day, the hunch that everything she's been working for isn't worth it.

"It does look good," Dove agrees. She considers the purchase. "It's been a long time since I bought anything like this." Scrimping and saving hadn't felt bad when she'd had a goal—to save up for the trip to see William. But now, with the reality of island life washing over her—and William showing little to no interest in being with her all the time the way she'd imagined—the penniless life feels less alluring.

The salesperson smiles, her bleached teeth nearly blue in the overhead lights. "Go for it. Treat yourself."

"I will," Dove says suddenly. "I *will* treat myself." She touches the necklace from William, hoping it holds a fortune of love after all, and then removes the headband, studying it as though it was more than a simple accessory. *I deserve this. It's not a giant thing, just a small treat for all the work I've been doing.*

Satisfied with her impulse, Dove heads for the cash register. With the band on the counter, the salesgirl goes to ring up the purchase. Dove's hand reaches for her back pocket and her eyes wander out the large front window to the side street where a few people stroll by. Suddenly she stops the salesperson. "Hold on," she says. "I see an . . . old friend—I have to go." Dove dashes to the doorway.

Confused, the salesperson clutches the band. "Should I hold it for you? Tell me your name."

Dove pauses, distracted by the view out the window. "Umm . . . Lily . . . I mean, Dove." She shudders, wondering why her old name slipped onto her tongue. "Just put it under de Rothschild."

The salesperson writes the request on a rectangular card and stashes it behind the counter. "We'll keep it here for twenty-four hours."

Dove nods, completing her dash out the door just in time to grab Max's arm as he heads up a few stone steps.

"Hey—where you headed?" she asks, breathless and still clutching his arm.

Max stares at her hand on his arm and then locks eyes with her. "Lily—hey. I'm just . . ." He looks up the steps to the raised storefront.

Dove reads the sign out front. "Floral arrangements?"

Max scratches his chin, nodding. "Yes. Just—picking up a few things."

"For the house?" Dove asks, thinking about the massive tables at the Sugar Hut and wondering if maybe Max's mother sent him out to pick up things for a dinner party.

"Not exactly." Max bites his top lip and leans on the wrought-iron railing.

Dove looks embarrassed. "Oh . . . sorry—I just . . ." *He's giving flowers to someone.* She pictures him choosing a gerbera daisy or a fluted lily and her heart dips. "Who's the lucky someone?" she asks, feigning cheerfulness. *It's not like I care that I'm not getting flowers. But it'd be nice if William had done something for me. Some gesture instead of just half-empty words. Maybe it wasn't just the boat that got stuck in the sand when he was supposed to get me at the airport. Maybe it was—*

"Want to come in with me?" Max thumbs toward the store. "I wouldn't mind the help." He puts his hand on her shoulder, sending a sparkle of excitement down her arm. "If it's not too . . ."

"It's not weird. It's okay." Dove follows him up the stone steps and into the cool darkness of the floral house.

Inside, galvanized buckets hold elongated stems. "Bird of Paradise." Max reaches for one. Dove shakes her head, kindly wrinkling her nose. "Too pointy."

Max laughs. "Oh, okay. As if that's a reason."

Dove shoves him. "It is. Too sharp. You want something that says . . ." She swallows hard, avoiding looking at him. He always made her feel she could say anything, dissect or analyze without sounding too academic, as William had said. "What exactly do you want these flowers to say?"

Max roams between a rectangular bin filled to bursting with tropical roses and a tall glass cylinder that holds a multitude of wildflowers in shades of blue and purple. "What do I want this to mean? What do I want these things to say?" He touches a rose. "Everything. Nothing. I don't know." He sits on a bench by a twisted topiary. "How do you make a statement mean what you want?"

Dove sits next to him, small beside his tall frame. In the cool air, the flowers stay pert and Dove is reminded of being with Max in the cold air at Les Trois Alpes. *How different everything was then,* she thinks. *I had so much to look forward to and my struggle was to keep myself away from Max. Now he's the one with some big plan—flowers, some girl—and I'm the one with no job, nothing lined up.* "You mean, like a grand gesture?"

Max nods. "Sometimes I feel like I can say what I want in writing or in words, and other times . . . I don't know. Kind of lame, considering how much my day-to-day life revolves around papers and reading. Maybe it's best to just act on something and present your idea without so much explanation."

Dove nods in agreement. "I'm all in favor of that kind of thing. Words are good—amazing. But actions, they're not just a supplement. I keep going back to *Romantic Theory: Love throughout Literature* by A. J. Samuels and that part about how grand gestures throughout history have been life-altering." She watches Max's face. "You know, that book that—"

Max breaks into her words. "I know the one." His face registers the name and his eyes light up for a minute. "Do you have that book here?"

Dove shrugs her shoulders, wondering if she should say no. "Yeah. I do, actually—pathetic though it may seem, as I'm not in any way, shape, or form connected to a class that's reading it . . ."

"It's not pathetic," Max assures her. He points to a bright purple flower. "What's this?"

"Wild iris," Dove says. "Why, do you want to borrow it or something?"

"The flower?" Max grins. "Yes, Dove. If I could borrow the book, that'd be great. I could come to get it now if—"

Dove hears the town hall clock ring, signaling that morning is officially turning into afternoon. "I should go."

"Back to work?" Max nods to the flower shop attendant and says, "I'll be back in a minute for my order."

Dove wonders what flowers he'll pick, which girl is the lucky recipient, if her comments meant anything or influenced Max's future floral purchase. "Actually . . . I have to get my stuff from the boat." She squints as she steps into the bright sunlight, looking for a second at Pulse and remembering her headband. "I'm not so much going back to work as . . . looking for it."

Max grimaces. "Oops. Sounds like a story."

"One I'd rather not tell just now." Dove heads down the steps. "But suffice to say I'm not only in need of work but lodging, too."

Max opens his hands as if he's offering her something tangible. "There's always the Sugar Hut." He puts one hand up like a stop sign. "Wait. Before you neg the idea. Melissa's there. It's platonic . . ." He looks at Dove.

But what about the girl? The flower girl? Am I really going to stay at Max's place while he plans some giant delivery of roses for some vixen? "It might be weird, Max. Considering our—"

Does he even remember how intense things got with us at Les Trois? Of course he does. I do. Only, how can he act so normal? The warm wind waffles through Max's hair, temporarily sending most of it to the other side of his head, which makes his green eyes stand out even more than they usually do. Dove notices gold flecks in them and backs away a bit.

"Our Past, capital *p*?" Max nods. "But it might not be. I mean, we were friends first, right?" He gives her a regular smile, a regular look, fixes her with an absolutely normal gaze.

Friends. The word rings in the air like bells and Dove, for the first time, feels it settle into her. *Friends.* "Right. Of course."

"So what do you say? Come by after you get your stuff and stay for as long as you like." Max turns to head back into the shop, his mind filling with ideas for the order. "And bring the book—I've been meaning to reread it."

Like watching a shirt float on the water's surface and then sink, Dove slowly feels herself pulled back to the moment. The moment where she and Max are friendly only, nothing more and nothing less. *Isn't that what I wanted after all this time?* she asks herself. Dove watches him go inside, wondering just what he'll decide to buy, and whom it's for. She decides to go see Melissa to talk it over.

21

"She said I have to pay it back," Harley says to Bug. His head is in her lap, the heated black surface of the volcano pockmarked around them.

"Isn't this cool? The whole island is conical," Bug says, shielding his eyes from the light to look up at Harley.

"I know. And fringed with golden sands. You told me that already." Her voice is laced with annoyance. "Did you even hear what I said?"

"I did. The vulture wants payback and she'll make sure you stick to it."

"Bug?" Harley pushes him off her lap until he sits up.

"What?" He brings his knees up so he can rest his torso on them. "Man, I'm beat." He looks out past their observation spot to the volcanic center and holds Harley's hand, absentmindedly playing with her fingers.

"Why haven't I been to your boat?"

"Huh?" He swivels to look at her, his face showing no signs of anything except his trademark relaxed grin. "What do you mean?"

"It's a pretty straightforward question. We've been . . . together . . . for a bit—"

"Speaking of which, I have something to discuss with you. Or to tell you." Bug stands up, shaking his legs out and brushing off a bit of dirt from his calf.

"Wait," Harley says. The day's issues still hang over her head, clouding her mood and making her want to clear everything up as fast as possible. "Don't switch the subject. All this time and I haven't once been to your cabin. Seen where you sleep."

He shoots her a wry look. "Maybe that's because I need my sleep in order to do my job, and if you visited me on board, I can pretty much guarantee I wouldn't get any shut-eye."

"Haha," Harley says humorlessly. "Really. Tell me." She pauses. "Or maybe I should just show up there sometime."

This makes Bug blanch, his cheeks suddenly paler

in the light than his tan warrants. "No—that's not a great idea."

"Oh yeah?" Harley feels a heaviness in her chest, a weight where only a few days ago there was a buoyancy. *I know this feeling,* she thinks, remembering finding the smallest of things—a tiny note—in her high school boyfriend's jacket pocket. She'd borrowed the coat and rummaged for a tissue, only to find a tiny scrap of paper that read *Miss you*. It was enough. "Bug—are you seeing anyone else besides me?"

He sits down. "Where's all this coming from?" he reaches for her hair, but she pulls away, gathering the locks into a bun at the nape of her neck.

"It just seems odd, that's all. Not to have seen your place when we've hung out virtually everywhere else this island has to offer."

Bug sighs, putting his hands on either side of her face. "Did you ever once consider that maybe I have no privacy on the boat? That as soon as I set foot on board I'm asked to do stuff, even if I'm not on duty?" He leans in and kisses her gently on the mouth. Despite her doubts, Harley feels herself pulled in by him. "I just want as much time with you as possible, and I don't particularly want to share you with whoever happens to be hanging out on the boat—above- or belowdecks."

Harley hears *belowdecks* and hopes no one besides her has seen his berth. Looking into his eyes so closely, she knows he's being truthful. "So, it's just me? I'm like this volcano?" She points to the mouth. "I'm your center, your—"

Bug doesn't answer her; he just pulls her in for another kiss. When they pause he speaks again. "Let the record show that I am officially going to spill my guts."

Harley's breath comes in and out in jagged bursts, her mind a whir. "Okay."

"I've got something big to tell you . . ." His face reveals a trace of nervousness that sends Harley's mind reeling.

Harley waits for more. "And?"

He raises one eyebrow and peers at her as he stands up and faces the heavy railing that overlooks the volcano's crevasses. "And when the time's right, I'm going to spring it on you."

Harley chucks a pebble at him and he catches it. "All that buildup and you're not even telling?"

Bug shrugs. "I will, okay? But I have to get back to the boat. Besides, we've got tons of time for talking later."

"Oh, yeah? When?" Harley asks.

"At the party. Emmy Taylor's, remember?"

Harley nods. "I almost forgot."

"Well, don't—it's apparently going down as the biggest deal of the season."

Not that I have anything to wear, and not that it matters, Harley thinks. She stands up, wondering why she still has a feeling of doubt with Bug, though he always strings her along to the next time they'll be together. Harley puts her feet into her sandals and looks again at the impressive volcano in front of her. Just because it hasn't been active for decades doesn't mean it couldn't suddenly churn fire and lava, right? Sometimes no matter how sorted out everything seems, you can feel rumblings that tell you change is brewing.

Harley throws another pebble over the railing, knowing that no matter what changes are in store, she owes more money than she can afford to, and has no prospects for paying it back.

22

"Not with the whole hand. Just with the wrist." Matty Chase demonstrates his technique. "Of course, I'm showing you this on a carrot and you'll be shaving bits from a white truffle." He gives a weary sigh and Melissa continues to watch him. "And white truffles are important because . . ."

"Because they are rare?" she suggests, trying again to shave just the slightest edge of carrot from the stalk.

"Because they retail for hundreds of dollars a pound?" Bob enters the kitchen from the back door, standing with his arms crossed over his chest. He gives a nod to everyone else in the room and reserves his smile for Melissa. "You ready?"

She glares at him and uses her eyes to motion to Matty, hoping Bob will understand. "Give me just a few more minutes, okay, Bob?" She adds extra enunciation on Bob, and he gets the clue, disappearing outside to wait for her on the beach.

"Sorry, Mr. Chase."

"Matty," he corrects. "And it's fine." He checks his watch. "You're two hours late wrapping up here, anyway. Why didn't you say something?" With his hands he gestures for her to go.

Melissa puts down her knife and unties her apron. She can feel dried sweat on her scalp, her hands ache, and her feet feel like two overinflated balloons filled with sand, but she smiles. "I love it here." She takes a breath. "And I don't mean that in a kiss-ass suck-up kind of way, if you know what I mean."

Matty laughs. "Glad you can clarify." He shaves a perfect amount from the carrot and hands it to her. "And I'm glad my instincts were right about you. Sometimes, you just know it when you see it."

Melissa nods, thinking as much about Bob as she is the job. "I guess that's what they mean by a gut feeling."

"See you first thing in the morning," Matty says as he shoos her out the door. "And have fun with your . . . friend." He looks to the doorway, where Bob has resurfaced. Melissa watches Matty as he stares at Bob. Bob motions to the beach.

"Thanks," Melissa says to Matty, but before she leaves, she tries one more time to get the slicing right. With only her wrist, she flicks the edge of the knife on the edge of the carrot.

"Perfect!" both Matty and Bob say at the same time. Melissa laughs, letting the surprise of two *perfects* wash over her as she heads outside.

"Well," Bob says as he leads her to the trolley stop. "Guys can be real jerks."

"I know," Melissa says, thinking back to her own boy-littered past. Not that much had happened in the way of love, but with Gabe and James back at Les Trois Alpes, there could have been more success, if only James hadn't turned out to be a slug. "So, do you think I should tell her?" Confiding in Bob concerning her awkward position with Bug Slash William and his two girlfriends had seemed the natural thing to do. In fact, Melissa was realizing, talking to Bob about just about anything felt easy.

"Tell *them*, you mean? Don't you have to tell Dove and Harley? Doesn't seem right to tell just one that her boyfriend's cheating." Bob kicks at the sand with his flip-flop. "You can't wear these in a kitchen." He flicks his eyes back to the restaurant. "Too many knife-on-the-foot incidents. Very unpleasant."

"Gross image." Melissa takes Bob's hand, thinking again about the mounting dread she has. How to tell Dove her steady love is nothing but a cheat? How to tell Harley that her island fling is using her—or not—but is a slime just the same? "Just be honest with me, okay? That's all I ask."

Bob squeezes her hand. "I'm so not that guy. The date-more-than-one-person-at-a-time guy. You may not have noticed, but I'm pretty focused when I want to be."

"Yeah," Melissa acknowledges. "Me, too, actually."

"I noticed that." Bob mimes Melissa's perfect slice. "May you one day try it on a black and a white truffle, often called *white diamond* and *black diamond*. Their weight is typically only one ounce. Thus the price tag."

"Again with the food trivia. How—or why—do you know about this stuff?" Melissa pulls at his hand until he turns around.

Bob shrugs, tugging on a ringlet that's escaped its ponytail. "Just interested in it, I guess." He looks down the road for the trolley. "Ready for our field trip?"

Melissa nods, grateful that Bob has planned an

activity to distract her from the cheating issues and the upcoming party, which the whole island seems to be planning to attend. "Just what I need to distract me."

Bob makes a face, looking behind Melissa at the beach. "You might want to get distracted right about now." He leans in and kisses her. Melissa melts, her heart aflutter, her insides and outside happy—until she feels a tap on her shoulder.

"Sorry to bug you," Dove says.

Melissa winces when she hears the word *bug*, and then again when she realizes Dove has no idea about the double meaning. "No problem. What's up?" She scans the road for the trolley but there isn't one to rescue her from the conversation.

"Not such a great day . . ." Dove's eyes pool with tears.

"Let me give you guys a minute," Bob says. He leans in toward Melissa. "You know what's right." Melissa nods. "I think I'll go rustle up some grub for our little trip." Bob strides off toward the restaurant.

"Don't make too much fuss," Melissa shouts. Then to Dove she adds, "I just don't want him causing problems with Matty Chase. I'll admit to you that every time I'm with Matty Chase I want to blurt out 'please hire me to work on your new TV show' even though I know he'd probably fire me for it." She watches Bob walk up the deck to the front of the tent. "Bob's so mellow and unafraid of authority—the opposite to me, I might add—but he's so lax I worry he'll say something to offend the staff in there."

"Well, you can't control other people," Dove says, shaking her head. "That's for sure."

Melissa watches a lone tear escape Dove's eye. *Maybe she knows. She does. She found out about William and his piggish ways and has come for comfort.* "So . . . did you want to tell me something?"

Dove nods, her eyes welling again. "It was so bad, Mel. I mean, bad the way you have a nightmare about not knowing anything on a test and have to sit through the final exam."

Melissa tries to follow. "I hate those dreams."

"No, no, this was real." Dove brushes her hair back from her forehead and wipes her eyes. "It *is* real."

Melissa nods, patting Dove's back empathetically. "So you know, then."

Dove looks at Melissa like she's crazy. "What? Of course I know. I was there. But what do you know? Has word spread already?"

"Well . . ."

"I'll kill Gus. Really."

"Gus?" Melissa pauses, truly confused. "Hold on. What are you talking about exactly?"

"I got fired today," Dove says. She goes from crying to laughing. "It's stupid, really. It was so bad it was comical. Or it would be if it didn't make me broke and sad."

Melissa's heart slams. *She doesn't know. She meant the job, not the boy. But I have to tell her.* "Maybe some things are for the best," Melissa says, starting to build up to the issue.

Dove considers. "Maybe. Maybe it wasn't meant to be. Like, there's a different path for me and if I'd done the perfect breakfast—one without the damn Tahitian vanilla—I'd never know the correct path."

Melissa nods, overenthused. "Right. Exactly! Sometimes you think you want one thing, but then you realize that thing's not everything you think it is. It fails you somehow and then you can find the right thing."

Dove watches Melissa as though she's giving obtuse driving directions, her hands flailing. "Wait. Now I'm confused. What are you talking about?"

Melissa falters, panicking. *Don't shoot the messenger,* she thinks. "You deserve the truth . . ."

Dove puts her hand on Melissa's arm. "So do you. And I was going to talk to you the other night but . . ."

Melissa races to find the words to explain the

cheating. "The problem is that I know that you think you love William—"

Dove puts her hand over Melissa's mouth. "Hold on. Let me say what I'm going to say or I'll chicken out again. And based on the crappy day I've had, I have to at least let this go okay."

Melissa swirls with worry. *If I don't tell her now I'll completely lose my nerve. She has to know about William and Harley.* "Dove, William is—"

"He's not Max," Dove says, staring out at the rocking boats on the ocean. By the water, people wade in the waves, kids dig in the sand, and the well-heeled lunch crowd exits the restaurant full of the best food on the island.

"What?" Melissa is agog at Dove's pronouncement.

"It's something I've been realizing. When I was at Les Trois, I kept comparing Max to William. Since I've been here I keep doing the same thing—but this time comparing William to Max. Or at least I'm admitting this now, because I haven't before. Not even to myself."

All of Melissa's reserve starts to dwindle. "So you don't feel the same way about William that you did?"

Dove half laughs. "It's so bizarre. I want to. But I guess I don't. Not that it matters."

Maybe she does know, after all. "Why's that?"

"Because he doesn't feel the same way," Dove says.

"So you do know." Melissa gives the same empathetic pat to Dove's back.

"Stop patting me. I'm not a poodle." Dove waves to Bob, who wanders up the beach at a leisurely pace, holding a bag of food. "Didn't know they did takeout."

Melissa furrows her brow. "They don't." *Please don't let him have annoyed Matty or anyone else.*

"All I know is that Max used to like me, even liked me when he flew here. Or maybe that was just an excuse." Dove shakes her head. "All I feel is that I've missed my window. For Max, for Oxford . . ."

Melissa nods, knowing she can't possibly tell Dove about William and Harley when she's already so muddled. Not to mention the fact that maybe Dove wouldn't care as much about the cheating now that she had gotten in touch with her old feelings for Max. "So, you've decided on Max?" *Finally, their saga would be over—complete. Not that I'm one to talk,* Melissa thinks.

"Don't you see? Don't you get it? He doesn't feel the same way about me anymore. I had my chance and I didn't act on it. And now he's off buying flowers for some girl I don't even know."

Melissa looks surprised. "Really?" *After all his*

moaning and mushy feelings, I'd be shocked, but then again . . . "Are you sure?"

Dove sighs. "You go off with Bob. I'll see you back at the Sugar Hut." She waves her hands in front of her face, creating a little wind. "I know—call me a glutton for punishment—but I took Max up on his offer for a place to stay. Seems like it's my turn to pine for him while I consider my future."

Melissa greets Bob with a kiss on the cheek, feeling very glad to see him and slightly overwhelmed by the talk with Dove, and concerned about the big bag of take-out food steaming in Bob's hand. "See you back at the hut then," Melissa says. Dove gets on one trolley heading toward town so she can collect her things from the boat while Bob and Melissa step on a trolley heading the opposite way.

23

Everything is too familiar and at the same time totally different. *The last time I was here I was in school,* Dove thinks as she climbs the wide central staircase to the guest rooms. The Sugar Hut. She can hear Max's family frolicking in the pool outside and wishes she felt like joining them. But though she'd thanked them for the offer, she heads instead toward her temporary room to relax. *Everything's temporary these days,* Dove thinks.

She enters the bedroom, feeling at once a sense of ease from the motion of the overhead fan. Draped over the king-sized bed is the sheerest of mosquito netting, giving the room an air of regality. The floor is terra-cotta tile, the walls clean white. Dove slings her bags onto the floor. From her backpack she pulls the A. J. Samuels textbook, thinking she'll bring it to Max's room and leave it waiting for him. As she stands up to find his room, she holds the heavy text in one hand. A slip of paper falls out, fluttering to the floor.

Dove picks it up, unsure if it's a receipt or a bookmark. *Neither,* she thinks when she sees it. Back at Les Trois, she'd met Professor Hartman, an important faculty member at Oxford, who'd been keen to have her study there.

That's it, she thinks. *That's the answer. This whole time I've been wondering how to fill in the blank of what happens next, when it was there all along.* She grabs the book and the number and heads out the door to find a phone.

Harley counts the cash she has shoved into the side pocket of her black suitcase. Enough for a ticket out of here, but not to pay the party fine and the Pulse bill. She runs her fingers over her cheek, tapping. *Where else could I work?* She thinks back to the stores she's been to, the cafés, wondering if she could perhaps try a beach job—working at the sunglasses hut or something. Then she feels defeated. *No way. I've hardly got the references for anything local. But what else?* Harley thinks about the rest of the year ahead, her year between high school and whatever comes next, and wonders if maybe the solution is closer than she thinks. She puts her money back into the suitcase and begins to cram in her clothing and shoes. *I'll get ready for the Botanical Gardens party with Melissa and Dove. Like old times,* she thinks. *Except that I have to tell Dove about her parents' being in town. And that I got busted for using her name at the store.* Then she thinks, *But Melissa did, too. So maybe Dove will deal with the bill and I'll be off the hook.*

This sets her mind at ease. *And when I go to the party, no matter what Emmy Taylor does to shake her funds in my face, no matter what lack of prospects I might have, I will have a fun time.* Then she reconsiders. *That is, depending on what Bug has to say. He could make it better than fun. He could make it perfect.*

"So, this is it?" Melissa creeps toward a stone bench and sits on it, her skin prickling with the emptiness of the place.

"Yep. The Eden Brown Estate. It's haunted." Bob comes up behind her and pinches her waist. Melissa screams, and then yanks him down so they're next to each other. "Don't freak me out like that. I have to tell you—I get scared really easily."

"Duly noted." Bob points to the house. "Then I probably shouldn't inform you that it's all true. The rumors." He puts on a voice worthy of a horror movie. "Supposedly this woman Julia Huggins was going to marry a man but on the day of the wedding the groom and the best man had a fight."

"A duel?" Melissa mimes jabbing at him with a sword.

"Yeah." He grabs her sword arm and wraps it around him.

"And?"

"And they killed each other."

Melissa sticks out her tongue. "Not a very happy ending."

"And is that what you want? A happy ending?"

Melissa nods. "So, what happened to the bride?"

"She went bonkers. Became a recluse. The mansion was closed. You can go in if you want. But it's totally haunted. Everyone says they can feel someone's presence there."

Melissa shudders. "Um, no thanks. I'll stay right here."

"With me?"

"I suppose," Melissa says.

Bob gives her a faux-serious look. "Ms. Forsythe, are you suggesting that I am your happy ending?"

Melissa pulls back, blushing. "Hey, I never said that."

"Fine. So what else could conspire to make your dreams come true? Aside, of course, from me—" He grins.

"Truth?" Melissa pulls her knees up to her chest. "If I could make progress at work. I know it's really soon and I'm not trained properly, but it's like I've found my calling." She breathes in the musty air, looking at the mansion. "And I know this is what I want to do. I have all these ideas—not just for cooking, though I like that. But for—" She stops herself.

"For what? Just say it."

"Okay, but you'll think it's silly. So . . . I've heard that Matty Chase has a new project, something that's sort of under wraps. And I just think—I could help with it."

"With his television show?" Bob asks.

Melissa's face changes. "How do you know about that?"

"Sorry to inform you, but celebrity chef gossip travels faster than bad restaurant reviews. It's common knowledge."

Melissa blushes. "Oh. Well, that's what I want to do."

"Cook on TV?"

Melissa shakes her head. "No. I'm not the kind of person to go on camera." She stands up, her voice passionate. "I want to help do the segment ideas, plan them out, create them, research them. . . . I'm not a natural in the kitchen, but I'm a natural problem solver, and I love food."

Instead of laughing, Bob nods, thinking. "So give me an example."

"How?"

"Say I'm the ultrasuave Matty Chase . . ." He laughs. "And you have one minute to impress me and convince me you're meant to be on television."

"Not on it. Near it."

"Fine. Go—" He snaps his fingers.

"I once had to throw a ball for hundreds of people—royalty included—and pull it off without a hitch. I did it outside, with food, drinks, and entertainment." She watches Bob nod, impressed. "Well, let's say it's summer and we want to do a picnic segment that doesn't bore the pants off everyone. We do themed picnics—the kids' picnic with sandwiches made with cookie cutters, stars, circles, that kind of thing. And a women's-night-out picnic complete with hypothetical questions and great finger food."

"So, you'd combine food with activities?"

"Sometimes. And other times, it would be more

standard—recipe and prep and easy-to-follow, charming instructions with celebrity guests."

"It could work," Bob says. "A bit rough around the edges but it might fly."

"And what about you, Mr. Beach Guy?" Melissa hesitates bringing up what Bob's plans entail, hoping that they somehow include her.

"Depends on the tide," he says, feigning an Irish accent. He looks at her. "But the truth of it is—and you did ask for the truth, right?" Melissa nods, her pulse increasing. "The truth is I'm leaving for New York soon. Can't stay in paradise forever."

"No," Melissa agrees, wishing she hadn't asked, and feeling her own paradise slipping away. "You can't."

24

"I feel so guilty," Harley says, whispering to Melissa in the cavernous bathroom at the Sugar Hut. Downstairs, Max is waiting for everyone so they can drive to the Botanical Gardens.

"You do?" Melissa puts on lip gloss in the mirror and watches intently as Harley slides into heels.

"I should have told Dove."

Melissa spins. "So you know?"

Harley nods. "Yeah. I saw them—well, I think it was them. Hard to miss the Lady de Rothschild, since she's basically a carbon copy of Dove. Or the other way around."

"They're here?" Melissa's voice rises with emotion.

"Shhh. Yes. And they're onto the Pulse situation. Thus, I am out of a job yet again."

Melissa takes all this new information in and feels doubly bad about not spilling the cheating beans to Dove earlier. "Harley?" Melissa starts, thinking she'll have the courage to tell her about Bug.

"Yeah?" Harley spins on her heels, making her flouncy dress twirl out. "Can I just say that the one bright spot in my otherwise bad couple of days is heading to this party? At least it's one thing to look forward to."

Melissa smiles a small smile, understanding and not wanting to break Harley's spirit. *Besides, I have my own worries.* When they'd left the haunted estate, Melissa's spirits had flagged. *He's leaving. And just when everything was going so well.* "I hope we all have fun," Melissa says, covering up any hint that she knows about wrongdoings.

Downstairs, Dove is all grins. She grabs Melissa's hand and pulls her aside. "I did it!"

"Meaning?" Melissa's had enough confusion for one night. She feels as though she's about to burst with knowledge.

"I'm going to Oxford!" Dove squeals, trying to keep her voice low. "But don't tell anyone."

"I already heard," says Harley, wrinkling her nose as a sorry. "I thought you were talking about me."

"Why'd you think that?" Dove asks. "But isn't it great? Next term—I'm there. Provided, of course, that I haven't burned all my bridges with my parents."

"Ready to go?" Max hails them from the entryway. "I'm on a deadline." He taps his watch.

Dove's smile lessens just a tad. *He looks amazing,* Dove thinks. *Like he did back at my birthday party last year, when I thought for sure we'd end up together.* "I'm ready as I'll ever be." She motions for Harley and Melissa to keep the news of Oxford under wraps and they agree with a subtle nod.

"So, did you find the textbook I left for you?" Dove asks, resisting the urge to link her arm through Max's as they crunch over the crushed seashells in the driveway on their way to the car.

"I did. Thanks for lending it to me. It helped."

Dove nods. "That's what friends are for," she says, biting her lip as she says the word *friends*. *Sure, I still have to tell William about Oxford and our impending breakup, but I'm not about to say anything other than friend to Max. He deserves to be happy. I just hope he knows what he's doing with the flowers.*

"You guys can all meet Bug tonight—finally!" Harley says when they're strapped into the car.

"Finally is right," Dove says. "I feel like you've been hiding him away."

Harley nods. "That's what I told him. It's time to get everything out in the open, you know?"

Melissa feels a ripple of dread come over her. *Open is one thing, open to the point of disaster is another.*

25

With nearly eight acres of lagoons, streams, and waterfalls, the Botanical Gardens are lush and fragrant with budding shrubs and billowing tubs of flowers.

Near the rose garden, a bronze statue of a mermaid is surrounded by orchids and set back from the water is a plantation-style great house with a tearoom inside that has views of the ocean. All along the entrance are cameras with flashbulbs blazing into the evening, reporters with news crews covering the event for entertainment shows, and various recognizable faces from the weekly tabloids.

Emmy was right—this is the party of the season, Melissa thinks. *If only I had nothing else on my mind.* A bright flash causes Melissa to cover her eyes.

"They caught us!" Bob says good-naturedly, hardly flinching at the bright light. He sees that Melissa doesn't like the cameras and points her in the direction of the grounds.

"Wow. All I can say is wow." Melissa takes in the sheer beauty of the land and view before her.

"Pretty special, isn't it?" Bob leads her toward the mermaid statue. "This is where you're meant to make a wish."

Melissa watches him, sadness creeping into her stomach even though she's so happy to be with him. "I'm not sure about wishes."

Bob looks disgruntled. "That doesn't sound like the Melissa I know."

"And who is that?" Melissa pulls her gauzy wrap tight around her shoulders, wishing it could protect her from not only wind but hurt, too.

"Someone who cares, who's passionate and funny and able to make the proverbial lemonade out of lemons."

Melissa frowns. "Like that trait's going to get me a shot at the TV show, right? Coming up next, folks, how to make iced lemonade."

"See? You're the best." Bob kisses her lips. Melissa wishes it didn't have to end. "So, what would your wish be if you—ahem—believed in wishes?"

Melissa looks up at the darkening sky, searching for stars and other wish-inspiring things. Then she comes back to earth. "You tell me."

Near the great house, Harley and Bug are entwined, their lip-lock seemingly inseparable.

"Wait." Harley pulls back. "Enough. I want to be in the party with you. Not just near it."

Bug laughs. "Feeling a little hidden, are we?" Harley nods. "Okay. Fine. Just . . . wait here for a second."

"In the swamp?" Harley looks to her right—a big pond—and then to her left, where there's a large clump of prickly flowers.

"It's not a swamp. And I'll be right back."

Harley stands with hands on her hips, waiting for him to return. *What's his deal? And what am I doing in the middle of a jungly flower bed?* She swats at a buzzing insect near her ear. *It's enough to make me wish for the frigid temps of the Alps.* She's about to leave and follow him, worried that her earlier suspicions will prove true, when she sees something glint on the patio by the great house. Is it a shard of glass? A mirror? Harley goes to investigate.

By the veranda, in the flicker of light from the grand torches, she bends down. A bit of decoration from someone's dress? A rhinestone? "A diamond!" Harley says aloud and stands up holding it. It could be fake, of course, but in her hand it looks real. And large.

"Oh thank heavens," says a voice. "You've found it." A small woman with white-blond hair tucked into an elegant chignon approaches Harley. "That is it, isn't it? I've been looking everywhere."

Harley turns. "Did you lose something?"

"Her wedding stone," a tall man with a deep British accent wearing a dinner jacket says. "The prongs are always coming loose."

Harley holds the stone out toward the woman. Then, seeing her delicate hand, and going back to the woman's face, she feels a wave of familiarity. "Mrs. de Rothschild? Um, Lady de—"

"Yes," the woman says, gratefully accepting the rock. Her cool exterior matches her facial expression—not cold, just reserved. "Have we had the pleasure of meeting?"

Harley shakes her head. *No wonder Dove always seems so graceful, so demure. These are people from a storybook.* "No, we haven't . . . but I . . . I know your . . ."

"This is the horrid girl I told you about," interrupts a voice that belongs to Mrs. Taylor. With aqua-colored heels and a matching dress, Mrs. Taylor's outfit is loud enough to match her voice. "Great salesperson, terrible work ethic. Surprised she even handed the diamond back to you," Mrs. Taylor snorts, her bright-pink-lipsticked mouth twisted into a frown. "She's the one who charged a fortune of items—all in your name."

The de Rothschilds do not react to this. Rather, they stand statue still and regard Harley with a look that is neither menacing nor pleasant, just expectant. Harley stands there with her mouth open, wishing she could somehow evaporate rather than deal with the oncoming storm.

"Dove!" William spins her around in the darkened air. He surprised her, coming to the entrance a bit later than they'd set up, and immediately pulling her away from the spotlights and cameras and into a more secluded area. "There's my girl."

"Hey," Dove says, dancing with him despite the lack of music. *He's adorable*, Dove thinks, taking in his summery sheen, his affable grin. *But what has he proven to me aside from the fact that thinking about someone can be more rewarding than actually being with them? Not that much.* With a sinking feeling, Dove realizes that when she tells him her big new plans, she might in fact be letting him down the way he has her. "Some party, huh?"

"You should see the scene by the great house. All lanterns and food and incredible champagne." He focuses on Dove, who looks over her shoulder at Max as he walks away from her in the direction of the great house and its expansive gardens.

"Listen, William, I need to tell you something . . ."

William nods. "Me, too."

Melissa accepts a forkful of Bob's food. "You'll love it," he says. "Not the sesame part, that's standard fare for tuna, but the tapenade. It's got figs in it." Melissa tastes the food and nods.

"So good," she says. "How can you tell they're figs?"

Bob shrugs, taking another bite from the ancestral china plate. "How do you know how to drive on the left here? You just know."

"Instinct," Melissa says, her arms covered with chills from extracting the same feeling and applying it to Bob. Being with him just feels right. She squeezes his hand and he returns the gesture.

Melissa watches Emmy Taylor in the limelight,

glad that her own comfort isn't based on people noticing her. "Fame isn't all it's cracked up to be, I don't think."

"Oh, no?" Bob licks his lips and glances at the herd of paparazzi. Noise erupts from their gathering spot by the trellised entrance.

Melissa tilts her head to see what the fuss is about, but can't. "It just seems so unreal. Not fake, but just based in this other reality that doesn't exist on the same plane as I do. We do."

Bob puts his plate on the buffet table, his expression downcast. "Melissa—you should probably be aware that—"

Bob's train of thought is interrupted by a burst of bright orange. Mimicking her brother's former bathing suit, his sister Bethany's evening dress is the same hue, only made from fine silk that shimmers in the lights, making her even more radiant than she had been at the rotunda.

"Hey, Melissa!" Bethany says, swooping in with a friendly hug as though she and Melissa go way back. "You look great."

Melissa looks at her own outfit, then back at Bethany. "You, too. Nice to see you." *And glad she remembers my name, if only because it means I don't blend in with all the other islanders who've been interested in Bob.*

"Took you long enough to get here," Bob says, ribbing his sister.

She shoots him a look. "Well, let's just say I had a variety of—ahem—fires to put out."

Bob looks apologetic. "Success?"

"Mild." Bethany stands on tiptoe, looking at the now very noisy paparazzi. "Speaking of which, Dad's waiting for you. And may I suggest that this time you don't offer up any excuses."

Melissa looks at them both. "Dad? Your dad's here?" *I had no idea they were on a family holiday.* Melissa's shoulders sag. *Maybe he is ashamed of me, or maybe he just can't face introducing me.*

Bethany turns to Bob. "You did tell her—"

Bob flicks Bethany's arm and cuts her off in midsentence. "No. And if I can offer up one final excuse—I'm in the middle of talking about figs with Melissa."

"It's fine," Melissa interjects. "You can tell me about figs another—"

"No," Bethany announces. "He can tell you about figs right now. And stop leaving everything for me to deal with." She drags Melissa by one arm and Bob with the other toward the now rowdy red carpet.

"I can explain," Harley says, pleading with Lord and Lady de Rothschild. *It wasn't my idea. It wasn't even anything I thought about doing until Melissa came in and—* Harley looks at the elegant people in front of her, knowing she has a decision to make. She can either blame it on Dove—after all, Melissa isn't known to them, they won't care if her name is sullied—or she can, for once, admit to her own shortcomings and face facts.

"Please try to enlighten me," Lady de Rothschild says.

"And I'll be standing here waiting for the truth to finally emerge," Mrs. Taylor says.

"Actually," Lord de Rothschild says after an almost unnoticeable glance from his wife, "I think we've more than got the situation under control. You should attend to your guests."

"But I . . ." Mrs. Taylor stumbles over her words, hating to miss the next round of potential gossip.

"Please do," Lady de Rothschild says. "We'll be over to the dance floor shortly."

Mrs. Taylor exits, leaving Harley alone with the upper echelon and her own decision. "I come from nothing," she says, saying it aloud for the first time. "Trailer park—you know, like something you'd see in an American film?" She looks for signs this is making sense. "Or maybe not. But anyway, not like you.

And not like anyone here that I've met." She sighs, looking at the partygoers. "Not that I'm envious. I'm not. And I'm not intentionally a bad worker. I'm just . . . learning the ropes here."

"And what have you learned?"

Harley twists her hair, fidgeting. "That I'm more of a visionary than a detail person." She thinks about the rotunda, how she threw the party together so quickly and so well. Permit aside. "And that even though I do have these lapses in judgment . . ." She looks at the couple and blushes, stammering. "I—I was—I did take some things. Or borrow them on credit. I know it was wrong, but I thought I'd just pay it back."

"Well, you will," Lord de Rothschild says. "I've settled the account."

"You have?" Harley grins, thankful.

"Now your debt is to us," Lady de Rothschild says.

Harley's body feels weighted, her chest dragging. "But I don't have a job. I don't have a—"

"Surely there must be some work experience you've had where you didn't burn every bridge?" Lady de Rothschild asks.

Harley considers. "I'm a terrible waitress. And I know nothing about kids, so babysitting is out."

"Where were you before coming to Nevis?"

Harley's mind flashes with images—the chairlift at Les Trois, the Main House there, the warmth of her ski jacket, the tiring but social work. "At a ski resort."

Lord de Rothschild smiles and nudges his wife, sharing a moment that only they understand.

"So . . . the thing is . . ." William stammers, looking at Dove's solemn face. "You go first."

Dove chews her lower lip. "Um, I think you should."

William pauses, temporarily jostled by partygoers trying to spot the famous faces on the red carpet. "Well, it's not the easiest thing in the world to tell you."

As he's about to speak, with Dove looking wide-eyed at him, Melissa happens by, still being pulled along by Bethany. She overhears the last bit of their conversation, her expression annoyed. "Thank God! Make sure he tells you everything, Dove!" Melissa shouts, on her way to the paparazzi. "And I mean everything!"

Relief floods over Melissa's face. "At least I won't be the bearer of bad news," she says.

"But I might be," Bob says as his frame becomes illuminated by the heated halo lights set up to maximize the star power.

Caught up in the crowd and cameras, Melissa reaches for Bob's hand. Bethany waves to someone, trying to surge forth into the crowd. "Come on, I see him over there." She pushes Bob and Melissa toward the biggest group of photographers. "Time to face the music."

"What's all this about?" Dove asks, sure that Melissa wasn't just joking around.

William looks over his shoulder. "It's just that I've been offered this job . . ."

Dove sighs. A job. Okay, me too. Sort of the same. "Which is . . . ?"

"A boat delivery. Up the coast of New England. I'll be there all summer."

Dove overlaps his words. "I can't go with you, William. I'm sorry. I just—I'm going to Oxford. It's been a long time coming and it's a decision I—"

A wash of reprieve comes over his face. "So you're not pissed?"

Dove shakes her head slowly. "Not angry. Just . . . it's weird, you know? How much effort we put into this and now . . ." She's glad to have one of those fading breakups. Not the explosive kind. "So we're okay?" William glances over his shoulder again. "What are you, on the lam or something?" she asks.

He shrugs her off, but then sees Harley, walking purposefully toward him. Nerves make his hands shake. "So, yeah, we're good and that's all. Okay. Bye!" He starts to walk off.

"Bye? That's it? Months of being serious and then long distance and then one word? *Bye?*" Dove is shocked. Even though she's ready for the split, and her heart's elsewhere, it still stings.

"Um, I just . . ." He looks at her and then over his shoulder again. Harley is only a little ways away, her hair catching the red glow from a lantern.

"Hey, Harley!" Dove shouts.

William looks crestfallen. "You know her?"

With her feet firmly planted on the red carpet, Melissa stares at the celebrity reporters, the fashionable masses all posing for the cameras. "What's going on?" she asks Bob.

"Remember the rumor mill? How I told you Olivia and all those guys at the restaurant liked you after all?"

Melissa recalls the conversation. "Yeah. How'd you know all that?"

Bob gives her a sorry look and kisses her mouth quickly, all of which is caught on film. "Dad!" he yells.

Melissa follows the shout and is more than surprised to see a very familiar face. Dressed in a clean chef's jacket and black trousers, Matty Chase looks every bit the elegant chef. "Robbie!"

Bob pulls Melissa to where his father is standing, a microphone catching every sound bite. The reporter leans forward. "So, this is the infamous Robbie Chase!" Bob grins sheepishly, still holding on to Melissa's hand. Agog, she can neither move nor speak.

"That's true—I am my father's son," Bob says, his eyes flicking over Melissa's to make sure she's okay.

"I thought you said names aren't important," Melissa whispers. Then in her mind she goes over all the names that have been mixed up in the past months. *My old crush thought my name was Mesilla and not Melissa. Harley never knew Bug's name was William. Dove's real name is Lily. And now simple Bob turns out to be Robbie Chase. I guess you never know what's in a name until you look.*

Matty slings an arm over his son's shoulders. "My boy here's the next big thing to hit the airwaves." Melissa's heart begins to pound.

"Is this a fact?" The reporter leans the microphone closer to Bob's face.

Bob nods. "Yep—all true. Despite my reluctance, my dad made me an offer I can't refuse."

"And just what is that, exactly?" Melissa pipes up in Bob's ear.

Bob turns to her, holding her close around the waist as the reporter films the whole scene. "Looks like I'll be heading to New York City to start filming *Chase Me*, a new show that follows me around the globe testing food, recipes—and adding in a bit of lifestyle hints."

Melissa swallows hard. *Recipes, travel, lifestyle. Pretty much everything I pitched to Bob myself. The pitch that was meant to land me a job.* She lets her hand go limp in Bob's.

"Sounds like a hit for sure!" The reporter glows.

Matty thumbs to Melissa. "And he's got her to thank for it!"

"And you are?" The reporter signals for the camera crew to keep rolling.

Melissa says nothing until Bob nudges her forward. "Um . . . Melissa. Melissa Forsythe."

"She's the ideas behind the scenes. A critical part of *Chase Me*," Matty Chase says.

"And," Bob adds, "she'll not only be planning where I go on the show, but coming with me."

Melissa grins, turning for the first time toward the camera. *This is it! This is the job I've been wanting. And the guy.* "Just wait till you see where we go first!"

"You pigheaded liar. How dare you insult me!" Dove spits the words at William.

"How dare you insult *me*?" Harley shouts at him, punching his shoulder. He doesn't cower, but stands there listening to them berate him.

"I will never forgive you. What a waste of time!" Dove feels tears spring to her eyes. *Not sadness. Frustration. All that time wasted on William when I could have just been by myself. Or with Max.* His name echoes in her mind. *Max.* "Harley—he's all yours."

Harley grabs Dove's arm. "Do you hate me?"

Dove shakes her head, looking at Harley's leggy body, her photo-worthy face. "You didn't even know. I'm not dumb enough to blame the other woman in this scenario." She glares at William. "This one's all on you."

Dove marches away, her shoes clicking on the walkway. Out by the ocean, boat lights blink on and off. *How glad I'll be to get back to normal*, she thinks, wiping the tears from her eyes. *No boats, no food prep, no pining for a boy I can't have.* Then, up ahead by the secluded orange grove, she sees Max. *Well, maybe my days of pining aren't completely finished.*

The air is scented with lime and lemons, and Dove removes her shoes to feel the lush grass underfoot.

"So lovely," she says when Max is in earshot.

Max turns, breathing in the sight of her and the air. "I thought you'd never show up."

Dove's brow wrinkles in confusion. "What?"

Max steps toward her. "You were right. About the flowers? Gerbera daisies were the way to go."

Dove studies Max, then moves her gaze to the surrounding flowers. What seems like millions of the daisies are set in swirling patterns.

Max climbs up on a stone bench. "Come here. You need to be elevated to get it."

Wordlessly, Dove trusts him and climbs up. She looks into his eyes, wishing she knew what all their history meant. "What am I supposed to see up here?"

"This." Max turns her face so she can view the flowers, but this time a clear pattern emerges. "It's . . ."

"It's the book!" Dove nearly cries. "The cover of my *Love* textbook. Only—" She peers closely in the night air. Enough light from the party casts rays over the flower heads. "Only—it's not a random couple." She looks at the purple flowers, the reds and bright yellows, the white forming the woman's slender hands. "It's us."

Max nods. Without explaining anything further, he slips his hand around Dove's, pulling her into him the way the couple is on the textbook's cover: entwined.

Shrieks and bursts of laughter, a mass exodus, and confusion all create a tornado of people running this way and that. A downpour sends everyone seeking shelter in the great house and under the food tents.

"Lily!" Lady de Rothschild holds her purse over her head but can't disguise her surprise at seeing Dove.

"Mummy!" Dove stops in her tracks and hugs both her parents.

"Your hair!" her father says.

"Chopped," Dove says, her insides doing cartwheels from Max, still prickling from William, and now caught off guard by her parents. *I won't bend down to them. I won't admit defeat. After all, I'm not defeated. I've grown. Changed.* "Before you get too soaked, let me get this off my chest—"

"We've heard," her father says, water streaming down his face like tears.

"Heard what?" Dove shivers. Then she frowns. "Fine. So you were right about William . . ."

"Who cares about bloody William?" her father asks.

"That's right. We're just thrilled that you've made the decision to come home. To go to Oxford." Her mother grips Dove's shoulder.

Dove bites her lip. "But how'd you find out?" She's so relieved that they're happy and that they're here that she doesn't mind not being the one to inform them. *In fact, it's easier this way. Whoever told must have known how hard it would be to admit that I was wrong and basically did it for me.*

"Your friend," Lady de Rothschild says. "The very steady and sweet Harley."

Dove's face rises with a grin. Harley. "There's more to her than you think."

Her parents nod. "It's good to see you again, Lily."

"Dove," she says. "Everyone calls me Dove."

This time, instead of insisting otherwise, her mother looks at her daughter's wet hair, her new self. "Welcome back, Dove."

In the middle of the torrential rain, Melissa finds Harley and Dove in the otherwise empty gazebo.

Drenched to the bone, Melissa laughs. "I've been looking everywhere for you guys!"

"Yeah, well, here we are," Harley says, sticking her hand out to collect a bit of rain and then whisking it through her hair. "All the money and power in the world can't stop the weather."

"Not even the Taylors'," Dove says, opening her arms up to the downpour. They sit there, clothed in soaking formal attire in the partial shelter, sticking their legs through the gazebo railings and trading thoughts.

"I can't believe I'm going back to school," Dove says. "University. Oxford. Work."

"Max . . ." Melissa suggests.

Dove grins. "And you—"

"I can't believe I'm going to New York City," Melissa says.

"It sounds amazing," Dove gushes.

Melissa nods. "And Harley—"

"I know," Harley says. "Good thing your parents have so much pull." Harley rests her head for a moment on Dove's shoulder. "I can't believe I'm going back to where the three of us met," she says. "Les Trois."

They each think back to their beginnings on the mountain and how far they've come.

"Think we'll see each other again?" Harley asks them both.

"I might just have to concoct a research paper on French mountain history," Dove says with a smirk.

"First of all, I still have to look for my luggage!

You never know what—or who—you might meet at the airport." Melissa smiles. "But we'll find out. I could see if *Chase Me* is interested in a segment about traditional food of the Alps. With a modern twist, of course." They stand there, in the rain, the skies overhead echoing with thunder and with possibilities.

About the Author

Emily Franklin is the author of the *Chalet Girls* books and the *Principles of Love* series, as well as the novel *The Other Half of Me*. Her two novels for adults are *The Girls' Almanac* and *Liner Notes*. She has edited several anthologies, including *It's a Wonderful Lie: 26 Truths about Life in Your Twenties*. She lives in Massachusetts with her family.